DO NOT REMOVE
CARDS FROM POCKET

BLUE

a novel by

denise

OHIO

mcpherson

BLUE

All rights reserved. For information, address the publisher:
McPherson & Company, P. O. Box 1126, Kingston, New York 12401.
Publication of this book has been assisted by grants from the litera-
ture programs of the New York State Council on the Arts and the
National Endowment for the Arts, a federal agency. Designed by
Bruce R. McPherson. Typeset in Palatino and Stone Sans by Studio
Graphics. Manufactured in the United States of America.
1 3 5 7 9 10 8 6 4 2   1993 1994 1995 1996
FIRST EDITION

Library of Congress Cataloging-in-Publication Data

Ohio, Denise, 1962-
    Blue : a novel / by Denise Ohio.
       p.   cm.
    ISBN 0-929701-37-2 (cloth) : $20.00
    ISBN 0-927901-30-5 (trade paper) : $12.00
    1. Afro-American women musicians—Fiction.   2. Family—United
States—Fiction.   3. Twins—United States—Fiction.   I. Title.
PS3565.H58B57   1993
813' .54—dc20   93-29091

Page 224 is a continuation of this copyright page for notice and
acknowledgment of permissions granted for reprinting song lyrics.

The paper used in this publication meets the minimum requirements of American
National Standard for Information Sciences—Permanence of Paper for Printed
Library Materials, ANSI Z39.48-1984.

For Bessie, Billie, Clara, Dinah,
Ella, Lena, Nina, Sarah and the rest.

Blue

The blues is a feeling and when it hits you,
it's the real news.

— Leadbelly

Prologue

The body bag zipping shut over Israellen Jones's face was the same color as the airport cop's raincoat—a hard bright yellow that glowed like a piece of the sun in the floodlights.

"Clear the area," the cop shouted at Rickshaw Jones. "Now!"

A drop of rain slid down her cheek like a cold, strange tear as the last ambulance, the one without any lights flashing, pulled away from the crash site. Wiping her face with the corner of her scarf, Ricki shook back her dreadlocks. The rain that seeped into the parts of her hair caused a cold ache. Liberty Grace, if you could see your ballerina now, Ricki thought, walking back to the terminal. She's gone, Liberty, burned away, her skin gone to lace, unraveling like the ends of a Spanish shawl and now she's gone, just like you.

Another cop waved her over to the portable stairs that lead to Gate 68, the place where she'd been standing when the plane turned into a ball of fire. People were silhouetted against the huge windows, sharp-edged shadows on the glass. Come to see the disaster, she thought. Almost as entertaining as a hanging and better than a car wreck. Fill your eyes with it.

The warmth eased her strange headache as soon as she stepped into the terminal. She could feel the stares, too. Ricki was used to being stared at; someone once told her it was because of her eyes, their color that of shining spring grass on an overcast day. Isra had said it was her hair—who expects a white girl to be wearing dreads that go to the middle of her back? But Ricki herself thought it was the shade of her skin; in the fluorescent lights of the airport terminal, to all the people staring, she was really and truly a white woman.

Sometimes a human being isn't exactly what she appears, Ricki wished to call out as she walked through the crowd.

"Hey, you're Ricki Jones, aren't you?" a young white man asked, suddenly walking in step with her. "I really love your music."

Ahead, she spotted the bright lights and camera flashes of the press. Vultures.

"Excuse me," the white guy said, "I think the TV cameras are over there. Maybe we should go another way."

Rickshaw stopped dead. "Thanks, but *we* ain't going anywhere."

Camera lights glared in her direction. Damn, she thought, glancing around. In five seconds they would be on her. These vultures, she thought again, would eat somebody alive if it made a better story. A thin man sweeping the floor bobbed his head at her.

"Come on, baby. I'll get you out of here," he said.

He leaned his broom against the wall. Pulling keys from the ring on his belt, he unlocked a door and walked through. "Come on. Don't worry about the sign; I am authorized personnel."

Ricki followed him.

"I'm Ted Willems," he said, locking the door, then touching the white oval name tag stitched to his blue coveralls. "But everybody calls me Speedo, like it says."

"I'm Ricki Jones."

"I know. I know that. Just follow me."

He moved quickly. As he walked down the narrow corridor his loose coveralls flapped against his thin legs. The sound reminded her of wind whipping through the clothes hung on the line in back of the house on Banfield Street. Liberty would

10

hang their laundry out to dry; in autumn the cold would freeze the towels.

They rushed down a narrow flight of stairs and took a sharp right. With every quick step, the ring of keys let out a sharp jangle as they bounced against his hip. His skin was a fine mahogany, same color as the back of my Martin guitar, she noticed, and darkened at the creases around his elbows and eyes. Ahead, two ladders lay against the length of the wall, and Speedo slowed to let her go first.

"Fire hazard, that is," he mumbled, stepping into the lead again.

He looks like Yaz, Ricki decided as she watched his face—narrow and smooth but for crow's-feet, a little loose skin in his neck. The white patch of hair above his left ear, oval-shaped like his name tag, gave no clue to his age. Fifty, maybe? Forty? They took another right, walking carefully around a sawhorse. Passing through an archway, they took another right and ended up in front of a huge steel door. He unlocked but didn't open it. "Somebody important on that plane?"

"My twin sister."

"I am sorry about that, baby."

He swung the door open. The orange lights from the parking lot filled her eyes.

"You drive safe," Speedo said. "You need anything, you call me. Just dial airport information and tell them you're looking for Speedo Willems."

"I will. Thanks."

"Now get going before those TV people show up."

Pulling up her collar, she walked fast to her car, feeling safe once wrapped in its tinted windows and black paint. She turned the rearview mirror in her direction. Her face, rectangular and pale, scowled at her. That doesn't even feel like me. With her fingers, she tried to loosen the muscles in her jaw. Her hands froze as she stared into her own eyes. Strange, they look smaller, as if my cheeks are pulling them down at the corners. She pushed the mirror back, leaned into the seat and turned the key in the ignition. The car started immediately, music from the radio roaring over the sound of the engine. Ricki slipped a cassette into the tape player. Sing to me, Bessie Smith.

I woke up this morning with an awful aching head...

Wish Liberty was here. Wish Emma'd show up with her beat-up guitar and a few good stories to tell. But they're all gone, they're all gone and there's nobody going to help me out of this.

"Except you," she whispered, driving out of the parking lot.

I woke up this morning with an awful aching head...

Ricki pulled onto the Crosstown Highway. How do they put the skin back on burnt people? Do they take it off dead bodies or what? Is there anything left of Isra for somebody to use, maybe her eyes or something? Ricki changed lanes and stepped on the gas. She probably wouldn't like it if I gave her away.

My new man had left me just a room and an empty bed...

Her skin is about the right shade for a Hmong, or an Indian. Just a little lighter than Liberty, still dark enough for people to see she was black. Mulatto. That's the word. Sounds like mutant. Ricki smiled. She'd love that, like she's got six toes or something.

Bought me a coffee grinder, got the best one I could find...

And Liberty was just a half-beat darker, like caramel. Like Siobhan. And Emma was really and truly the color of chocolate.

Bought me a coffee grinder, got the best one I could find...

Then there's me. Dishwater blond hair and green eyes. Christ. Talk about mutants. I don't even qualify as high yellow, Miss Bessie. What would you say to that?

So he could grind me coffee, 'cause he had a brand new grind...

One

"I'll meet you on the beach, okay?"

Israellen nodded at her sister and began walking. Siobhan had said Three Cliffs Bay was the most beautiful place in Wales and she was right. Who cares if she and Ricki have a casual thing going? Just get me to the water. It's the last day Ricki can spare and the only day we'll be on the beach.

Isra rubbed her bare arms and walked faster down the gravel path leading into the sand dunes. The wind pushed her long black hair out of her face and ruffled through her thin cotton shirt. Good idea, Ricki going back for sweaters; we're going to need them. It's chilly at the seaside in the middle of May, though the sun is warm. Isra tilted her face towards the light. The setting sun mixed with her skin, her face gold like a flame. This feels wonderful. I hope Ricki enjoys it, too. She looks good now. These three days have helped get back the little color she has. Eighteen cities in twenty-two days is enough to wear on anybody, even my sister the superstar. She looks happier than I've ever seen her. Must be Siobhan. And the music, of course. Music's always been her cure, more like her blood than her blood really is.

I don't want this time to end, she thought suddenly. We've had only these three days in the four years since Liberty's been gone. Seems I lost Ricki long before that, though. I'm only twenty-five years old, how did I lose both my mother and my twin? Liberty died. That's the fact. Then Ricki and I separated in every way. Now I want them back. I want Liberty's worry and Ricki's carelessness. These last three days have fallen on me like an enormous yes. This is what I want. Whether Caleb wants to be a part or not.

A cold breeze rippled through Isra's shirt again and tangled her hair.

Caleb. He has no say. Maybe he should, but he doesn't.

At the edge of the path where the gravel stopped and the sand began, Isra glanced over her shoulder. I could wait for Ricki here, she thought. She shifted, the small stones of the path grinding together as if happier to be pushed into one another than kicked away and separated. Unsteady ground, Isra thought idly, watching a sand devil spin ahead of her. I shouldn't walk alone on such unsteady ground. She tensed her left knee over and over, an old habit. Each movement caused an ache. After all these years, she'd be amazed if there was no pain; she almost welcomed it as a reminder of everything that's happened before now. Sometimes, when I'm standing in one place and thinking of another, I feel like I'm living in both at once without regard for time or distance.

Isra shivered and crossed her arms, trying to hug in some warmth. I'm not used to being cold anymore, she thought. This is nothing compared to Minneapolis in January.

A thin layer of ice under the loose snow meant trouble for a woman with a bad leg. Jaywalking at the corner of Fifth and Banfield, Liberty Grace Jones stepped precisely into the footprints she'd made on her way to the bus stop that morning. Lewises still haven't shoveled their walk. If the snow piles any higher, I'm not going to be able to see the traffic, and that'll be the day I end my forty-eight years on earth beneath the wheels of an MTC bus. Then who'll take care of my girls?

As Liberty walked, cold branched up her legs like a tree beneath her skin. Gripping the ends of her scarf tighter in her mittened hand, she moved carefully. Always worse in the winter, she thought, my ankle feels stiff, like the bones weren't meant to move in the first place. I got a right leg full of reluctance. Pulling her elbows in closer, she tightened the muscles across her back and shoulders. Too much moving and her gray wool coat might open somewhere, letting the cold get a grip on her like the one she had on her scarf.

Funny how when it gets dark so early a person starts thinking about the sun and all the times it's burned into every crevice of skin, she thought, stepping slowly around a mysterious lump in the snow that may be a forgotten tricycle. For that one second it all comes back—in less time than it takes snow to melt on bare skin, it comes back to life. Maybe that's what eternity is: if you remember back as far as you can, you breathe life into all those people, then they turn around and start remembering as far as they can and on it goes, ricocheting through centuries. Not just backward either. Sideways, upside down, maybe forward. There's a special kind of magic called inheritance. My daughters didn't just get their mama's long hands and knock-kneed walk. From me they get dreams, wishes, the lines that will etch their faces and the way they fall in love. Time won't change that; it'll just keep adding layers, intricacies and movements as old as memory itself.

Time is like a ball of yarn that a kitten has gotten into. Ragged, unexpected bits of thread intertwine, making people and emotions and memories knot up. Cats definitely have an understanding with time—they seem to see everything that ever happened or is going to happen in one particular spot. Maybe that's why they sleep so much: all the activity wears them out. And maybe I've been walking in the cold so long my brain has started to freeze. She glanced down the street at the house. A shadow in the window. Well, one of my girls is home.

A tattered piece of red, white and blue ribbon flapped on the Dead End sign. One of Mrs. Dropik's boys had tied it on to celebrate the Bicentennial two and a half years ago. In the streetlight, it looked red, white and black, the colors Mamie

Fortune had thought the American flag ought to be. America is worse than Hitler, she shouted on the Fourth of July 1945, Liberty's fifteenth birthday. White people torture us, make us suffer with no jobs, no money and little dignity, then write about freedom and democracy in the morning paper. They might as well put a big sign next to the American Dream: no Negroes need apply. Wonder if Louise Dropik would appreciate that, Liberty thought. Wonder what got me thinking about Mamie? Seemed to happen before I could stop it, this rushing of wish and memory like a flood. Cherise used to say remembering is like water—human beings can die thirsting for it.

She smiled under her scarf, her face stinging because the cold made her skin dry and ashy. Wonder which one is home. Isra's turn to cook. Be nice if it was something other than Spaghetti-O's. A woman'd think her grown daughter would be able to handle more than that for a meal.

Liberty walked to the small white house with black shutters, the last at the bottom of the street. Looking as always like a shoebox with a roof, its porchlight burned warmly in the cold evening as she trudged down the driveway to the back door.

"I'm home," she called, stepping into the warm kitchen. She closed the door and took off her mittens. "Ricki? Isra?"

Liberty flipped the switch for the light, then leaned over the kitchen table to turn on the small radio near the toaster. Disco music drifted into the room. The only good thing to come out of disco is Patti LaBelle, she thought, quickly turning the dial to WCCO and the six o'clock news. She took off her coat and stuffed her scarf into the right sleeve. These mittens, she thought as she pushed them into the coat pockets, are quite a find. What a Christmas present, along with the electric socks.

"They'll keep your feet warm. See, clip the battery pack to the top of your new boots," Israellen had explained.

"I'll get electrocuted."

"No, you won't," Ricki jumped in. "You're not grounded."

Liberty shook her head, set the white box from her lap to the floor and opened the next gift. Goose-down blue mittens with red racing stripes across the backs. She picked up one and stuck her hand in it.

"You like them?"

"We got the receipt if you want to bring them back," Isra offered.

"She won't bring them back, she don't bring anything back." Isra rolled her eyes. "She doesn't want to hurt your feelings. You always pick out the stupidest presents."

"That's enough," Liberty said automatically. Twins, ha. Twins are supposed to get along, they're supposed to be alike. Couldn't be two people more different than my girls. Israellen, black eyes and hair balancing her perfect skin the color of oak leaves. And Ricki, green-eyed with light brown hair in all those stringy knots, sitting on the arm of the couch sucking on a candy cane. "Get off there, Ricki, you're going to break the sofa."

Sitting down on a kitchen chair, Liberty unzipped her boots. To think I was ashamed to wear mittens since that day Emma Nevada got pearl gray dress gloves in fifth grade. From then on, Emma'd rather have her fingers turn actually and truly white from frostbite than ever wear mittens again. She thought she was such a grown-up. And she teased, god, how she teased. I knew I wouldn't get gloves like that, ever, though I begged and begged. Tap shoes or fancy gloves, Cherise had said. Pick one, you can't have both. I thought those gloves would look so fine; Emma had let me try one on as we were walking to school that morning and my hand looked so beautiful. Cherise said if I chose the shoes, she could teach me a living. Mamie said Cherise would be better off teaching me how to move my ass—I'd certainly make more money going into Ruthie Nevada's line of work. Then she poured herself another drink. She was warming up for the fight that would last till Sunday, when she'd come home, say she was sorry, and she and Cherise would disappear into their bedroom, leaving me to turn up the radio to drown out the sounds they'd make.

"Hi, Liberty," Israellen said, limping into the kitchen.

"Girl, will you ever learn not to sneak up on people?"

"I didn't sneak up. You were shouting for me."

"I wasn't shouting, just wondering who was home. Help me with these boots, will you?"

Isra leaned over and grasped the heel of one. "How's the leg, Mom?"

"I should be asking you that."

She shrugged and began to pull.

"We started Winter Session at the dance school today," Liberty said.

With another tug, the second boot was off. Liberty stood up and tucked the pair by the radiator under the table.

"All those nice little white girls in their new leotards and hair ribbons," she continued, gathering up her coat. "One of the grandmothers even had the nerve to tell me her granddaughter is as talented as that little Shirley Temple, you know? Even looks like her, the little darling," she mimicked, grabbing the mail from the kitchen table as she walked to the living room.

"Want some pop?"

"No thanks, honey. That stuff rots your brain."

"What did you say to her?" Isra asked, grasping the back of a kitchen chair.

Bills. She dropped the mail on the end table and opened the closet near the front door. "I agreed—telling the truth would've got my butt fired. But let me tell you, that is one ugly child."

Isra inhaled deeply. First position. *Grand battement.* Leg straight. Body aligned. Feel the position.

Liberty hung up her coat and closed the closet door. "So she scooped up her little Farrah or Tiffany, I swear white people got funny names, and she says to me, 'My, but you people can dance.' "

Point. Chin up, Israellen commanded herself silently. *Battement.* Higher. Higher.

Yep, the world is still a mess, Liberty decided from the front page of the *Minneapolis Tribune* on the coffee table. "I wanted to tell her, my, us people can walk, too, even when it's twenty below, but even us people would rather have a ride to the bus shelter in your big heated Lincoln Continental than go outside to prove the ability."

The cat curled on the rust tweed recliner opened her marigold eyes and gazed up as Liberty reached over to pet her. Cat looks nice there. I can remember Big Henry carrying in the chair, bitching and moaning like he was going to break his back. Said it was a worthless piece of junk because of that tear in the back. But show business taught me more than how to flash my tits—I mended the rip and it held up till just last year, when I got it reupholstered to match the rest of the room. "Hello, Tina Turner," she cooed to the cat.

Grand battement, dammit, get it right, Isra demanded.

First piece of furniture I ever bought was this stereo, Liberty thought, running her hand over the wood. Bought it at Montgomery Wards when I first moved in and been playing it ever since.

Isra's leg started to ache in a half-moon below her knee. *Battement developé, a la séconde.* And again. Correct placement. Eyes front. Align the body. Bend. Straighten. The hips must never be sacrificed for high extension.

Liberty flipped through the record albums stacked on the stereo console. *Birth of the Cool, Milestones, A Love Supreme, The Americanization of Oogabooga, Young, Gifted and Black, Django*— why can't Ricki ever put things back in order? she wondered, skipping past Israellen's copies of *One Nation Under a Groove* and *Everybody's Dancin'*. "What is this?" she called out.

"What is what?" Isra called back.

"*Never mind the bollocks here's the Sex Pistols.* What kind of music is this?"

"I don't know. Ricki bought it."

Of course, Liberty thought with a shrug. Under Bob Marley

and the Wailers' *Natty Dread* was the Billie Holiday she was looking for. Putting the record on the turntable, she set down the album cover and walked into the kitchen.

Lady sings the blues...

"Israellen, what are you doing?"

"Nothing."

Liberty pushed the straight-backed chair to the table. "Dinner ready?"

"Almost. Did you dance today?" Isra asked quickly.

"A little. I dance every now and then." Liberty opened the refrigerator and grabbed a can of V8 sitting next to a head of lettuce. "Long as I don't overdo it, know what I mean? Everyday workout is fine, but not with an injury."

Isra bit her lip. "Yeah. I know what you mean."

"If Emma Nevada was here, she'd smack you for stretching out. She threatened to do it to me almost every day even if I was just walking."

She's got 'em bad...

"Why don't I start your bath water for you?" Isra suggested.

She's trying to hide that limp now, Liberty thought, following Isra out of the kitchen. But I can see it. Poor kid. Eighteen years old and she's already lost her first love. Sweeping the cat off her recliner, Liberty sat down, raising the built-in footrest. It is a shame, Isra worked so hard, ballet was all she wanted. Madame Anderhazy was confident she'd make it, hell, we were all sure. Liberty sighed. I understand that disappointment; my own dancing days ended almost the same way but at least I had a lot of fun before then.

She feels so sad...

Setting the can of V8 on the coffee table, Liberty picked up a small box. A simple border of touching diamonds was carved into the lid and varnished to shine. Sort of the way Isra does, Liberty thought. Inside, a slim, sitting cobalt blue cat lay in black velvet. She lifted out the two pieces, the broken edges gleaming like obsidian, and fitted them together. The cat fit comfortably in her palm. I could fix it again, Emma Nevada, I certainly could, but I keep it for when you decide to come back.

"Wait till we get to St. Paul before you open it," Emma had said gruffly, handing her the wooden box on the train from Oklahoma City.

"Girl, what did you give it to me for if I'm supposed to wait?" Liberty said grumpily. Her left foot ached from having to support all of her by itself, the crutches made her armpits itchy and the three pillows Emma managed to get from a porter kept slipping from under her right leg. She glanced at Emma's face. Five-foot-ten Emma Nevada was a column of contradictions. "Oh, all right," she said, holding the small box in her lap the entire way to the St. Paul train depot.

They stood it on the mantle next to the clock in Emma's new one-bedroom apartment on Rondo Street. It was a dark place. Emma added ten lamps; a fire hazard, Liberty was sure, but even the brightest lights couldn't push back the winter evenings. She settled into the chair and turned on the radio. Ray Charles was moaning his way through "What'd I Say." Liberty liked Ray Charles. She liked Johnny Ace and Fats Domino, too. Emma thought Chuck Berry was something else, but she thought there was something missing in his style—too much business, not enough fun. Etta James was in a class by herself and a person could always count on B. B. King, no matter how tired he was, to put on a show. She and Emma had snuck down to an after-hours joint in Tupelo after their own show with the Travis James Revue to hear him. He played "Every Day I Have the Blues" while looking at Emma with every note.

Liberty propped her right leg on the ottoman. Nighttime just keeps throwing blanket after blanket of darkness over the houses until even Ray Charles can't give the gloom a shove—if he can't brighten up a room, who can? She unfolded the *Minneapolis Spokesman* she'd found last night under the big bed she shared with Emma while looking for the little silver clip that she needed for her ace bandage. Damn thing's always getting lost, Liberty thought, smoothing the yellow paper flat.

Wake up in the middle of the night with one of its shiny little teeth biting you in the behind.

The paper smelled dusty and felt as soft as skin in her hands. Two months sitting in this light-tight apartment, I've read everything but the labels on the soup cans and even those are looking interesting. At least I got this newspaper now—thank god Emma's a little forgetful about housecleaning.

She sang along softly with the Rinso White commercial. Emma'd go to the library if I asked her. We could just take the streetcar as long as the walks are shoveled. Emma Nevada is a good woman. We always stuck together. Maybe because her mama, Ruthie, and Cher and Mamie weren't exactly respectable. A whore and two bull daggers. Liberty shuffled the paper as if trying to get the newsprint into order. Ugly words, words Emma explained when we were seven that locked us into being pals from that minute. Then Emma taught me about Jesse Owens, and I taught her how to dance on that big flat rock near the creek. Fair trade. And it was Emma who started dreaming out loud how we would dance at Carnegie Hall, New York City.

Oh, good song. Liberty turned up the volume.

Good golly, Miss Molly...

And Emma still dreams, making me do those therapy exercises and soak my ankle in a pan of hot water, Epsom salts and a shot of whiskey. Keeps you from stiffening up, especially if you partake directly from the bottle, she tells me.

Sure like to ball...

Smelling of cold and still in her boots and coat, Emma dumped a paper bag into Liberty's lap.

Good golly, Miss Molly...

Liberty turned down the volume till Little Richard's voice was a tin whisper. "I didn't hear you come in."

"You're going to go deaf listening to music that loud." Emma nodded her head at the bag. "That's for the costumes."

Sure like to ball...

"What costumes?" She dropped the *Spokesman* onto the floor.

Emma pulled off her gloves and stuffed them in her coat pocket. "You shouldn't read that paper, Liberty Grace; they won't write about you unless you can see your veins through the skin of your wrists."

"Why do you have it then?"

When you're rockin' and a-rollin'...

"I like to know what the other side is up to." Emma shrugged out of her coat and tossed it on the couch. "Are you going to open the bag?"

Inside were folded yards of shiny red satin. Liberty pulled out the material and rubbed her hands over its smoothness. Soft, slippery and red like a person could warm up just by the color alone. She looked up. No wonder they tease Emma about her deer eyes, she thought. Even when she's trying to hide them they are clear and beautiful.

Can't you hear your mama call?...

"For when you start dancing again."

"How much did this cost you?"

Emma lit a cigarette. "How you know I bought it?"

"Em—"

From the early early morning to the early early night...

"You can sew the outfits while we wait for your leg to finish healing."

"Emma—"

"Make yourself useful. Then we'll find the gang."

"But—"

"Billy Wayne's in town at the V. A. Hospital," she rushed. "Toby and Thomas are around. And I know Jaylene and some of the other girls want to get together. Take a few months—"

You can see Miss Molly rockin' in the house of blue lights...

"Emma Nevada—"

"Think Will would want to come along?"

"Emma." Liberty finally broke in. "Stop it."

Emma inhaled again and crossed her arms. As she breathed out, the smoke rushed into the dim room. Her eyes were soft as velvet. "You're not going to dance anymore, are you?"

Good golly, Miss Molly...

Liberty shook her head and turned off the radio.

"Not even a chance?"

"No," came the soft answer. "Not on a stage."

Emma sighed. "What are you going to do?"

"I don't know."

Emma paced the line where the frayed carpet met the hardwood floor.

"Okay," she said finally, stopping as if she'd come to a decision standing in her way. "Okay. You stay with me as long as you want till you find out, okay?"

Liberty nodded. God bless you, Emma Nevada.

"But it's only temporary. I don't want no freeloaders in my house, got it?"

"Got it."

Three months later, Liberty was an heiress. A crumpled envelope with a crumpled letter and the deed to Bubba Jones's farm fell into Liberty's lap as she sat at the bottom of the steps leading up to the apartment. I'll be damned both ways and back, she thought, holding the pages in her hands. A farm. What am I going to do with a farm?

"What you going to do, Liberty Grace?"

"Sell it," she answered, handing Emma a letter to mail. That night she lay in bed, staring at the ceiling. From the open window came the sounds of the night, the parties in the corner apartment building, the harsh, loud laughing of the men on the porch next door. The night was cool and smelled like wet grass; spring might definitely be on its way, Liberty decided, hoisting herself up to the window above her side of the bed. The chill made goose bumps push out of her skin, and she pulled her nightgown tight around her. Outside, she could see the small knots of people sitting on the hoods of cars and standing on the walk. So glad not to be freezing to death.

Standing around in thin coats shows their faith in summer. Liberty shut her eyes. The summer grass in St. Paul had been emerald green, and the lilac bush Bubba planted in the backyard smelled like love itself. She could still feel the grip of his hands like the clasp of an old iron gate on her wrists as he swung her around and around.

"Careful," Mamie called. "Don't want her losing her lunch."

They spun and swooped and she was so happy she thought she'd blow up and bust. Bub slowed down and they glided to another landing.

"Once more," eight-year-old Liberty begged. "Please? Once more?"

Bub wiped the sweat off his forehead and whistled.

"That's enough," Cherise called from the porch, holding out a sweating can. "I don't want you getting sunstroked in this heat. Bub, come here and get you a Grain Belt."

But now Bub is dead and buried in some segregated graveyard in McComb County. And the letter said he died somewhere in New Mexico riding the freight cars. I wonder if he expected me to live in Mississippi. He couldn't have. Not the South. With the money, I'll buy another house to make a home in. I think he would've approved of that. Just like Bubba to give me free land, free money, no debts, he'd understand; he himself even managed to save enough money for his own funeral so there'd be no expenses. Started saving after the war and never touched his funeral money but for one go-round with Ruthie and an armful of groceries for us every time he came to town.

She glanced out her bedroom window at the people below. Wonder what they would do? Sell, just like I did. What is land to a bunch of city people?

A man spat in the gutter. She pulled away from the window, then realized that none of the neighbors could see her; who looks above the first floor when they're peeping in somebody's house anyway? A sudden ache began in her arms, just below her skin. Strange feeling, like my arms want to reach right out and hold somebody, pull them as tight to me as I can. She leaned back against the windowsill.

The lights on the porches and the streetlamps silhouetted the people. A shapeless man dropped his head back to laugh. What a roar he has, she thought, starts off a guffaw and ends up on a high note, like each bellow has to hit a note on the scale. Cherise laughed like that. Bub could only let out a giggle. Mamie hardly ever laughed at all, except when she was drinking. During the summer, she'd sit on the porch smiling her tight-lipped smile and watch the goings-on. Music drifted up to the bedroom window on a puff of wind, a song Liberty couldn't quite catch. Ella Fitzgerald, Billie, maybe. Rubbing her arms, she climbed back under the covers.

Lady sings the blues...

"You're blue, Tina Turner," Liberty said, looking at her through the two halves of the cobalt statue. Such a small beautiful thing. Seems I got just about the most beautiful things in my life because of Emma Nevada. Except my girls.

She tells her side...

I'd no more than hung the curtains in this house when Emma decided to leave and the gang split up. Billy Wayne and Thomas hit the road with Chuck Berry. Jaylene moved out of her apartment on Penn Avenue, sent a postcard from Hollywood, and I haven't heard from her since. It was as if Emma was the glue that stuck us together. When she left, the bonds started to dissolve. Emma would return when she needed to; after all, this little house was her home. She'd scribble a letter when she thought of it and I'd get it months later when she remembered to mail it. Creased, dirty, words fading in places, at least I had a lifeline to her. Letters can do that. But gone is gone and Emma left. Searching, she said, for new adventures.

"New adventures? Being broke for ten years and traveling with a bunch of two-bit show people didn't give you enough adventures?" Liberty shouted as she climbed into the driver's seat of Henry's Chevy. "Come with me to see Bubba's farm. That's adventure. We'll go to Mississippi, then come home."

Emma laid her hand on Liberty's arm. "I can't, Liberty. I'm expected somewhere else."

Liberty looked into Emma's eyes, a bolt of fear flashing through her. "Be careful, Emma."

"Look who's giving me advice." Emma's sudden grin faded. "You're the one who should be careful, Liberty Grace."

Emma then warned her to add water often because the radiator had a leak, and Liberty had to stop for water six times on her way to Mississippi and back. When she returned the car to Big Henry, he glanced at the odometer and shook his head. He only lent it to her because Emma lied and said Liberty had to go to Rochester to get her leg operated on at the Mayo Clinic. If I was Emma, he'd be shouting loud enough for three square blocks to hear him. But her running off to find new adventures as if they're waiting to be discovered like buried treasure has subdued Henry, Liberty thought, opening her purse to get a quarter for the bus. It's almost unnatural, how quiet he is about her.

Nothing to hide…

Other than Emma, the only one who wrote to me was Will. Strange man, Will Ross. A man born lonely. Being an only child growing up on a farm in North Dakota can do that to a person. Imagine not having anybody to talk to but a cow. Does wonders for a person's conversational abilities.

His next-to-last letter came on February 10, 1960. "Where did this boy learn to spell," Liberty mumbled in the empty living room, which was what she always said after getting a letter from him. She figured out he was on his way into town, of course he's welcome, shrugging into her coat and kicking her way through the snow to the liquor store for a twelve-pack of beer. The latest winter storm slowed everything—the mail, the people she passed on the sidewalk, the Greyhound bus carrying Will to Minneapolis. She didn't know when he'd be at her door.

"You're rounder," he said over a beer, once he showed up. "You were just a slip, real thin. You're still thin, but rounder, more curved."

"You haven't changed." It was true. Broad back, shoulders wider than his hips. She could remember the way his muscles bunched beneath his clean white t-shirt as he changed a flat tire. He moved quickly on the deserted Arkansas back road because a white man and a black woman in a truck with outstate plates were targets in that country. I love you, he had said suddenly, balancing the spare tire against his knees. I love you, Liberty Grace.

"And you look happier," he said, his voice pulling her out of 1956 and back to her living room.

"I am."

There was a pause as they both listened to the wind howling outside.

"What's this?" He tapped the wooden box on the end table with his finger.

"Emma gave it to me," she said, opening the box to slip the cat out of the velvet and hold it up. "See? You can look through it. Turns the whole world blue."

"It's pretty."

Liberty watched him through the glass cat as he shifted in the recliner that was almost too small for him. His strong, rectangular face and his blond hair reflecting the snow were awash with blue.

"I missed you when you left the show. First Emma, then you."

"She's in Birmingham."

"I know," he said quietly. "I'm going, too."

"I figured."

Will shrugged and smiled at his beer. "What do you think about all that?"

"I hear the commotion on the radio and hope it will all end."

He nodded. "You know, I'll never know how to thank Emma for dragging you into the Revue."

"She came up to Rondo after Cherise died, said there was a job in show business waiting for me."

"Not many people have friends like that."

"That's true," Liberty agreed. "Not many do. And she stuck around the Travis James Revue to look after me till I could look out for myself."

The two women stood just inside the dingy blue-and-white show tent.

"Like I told you before, don't be running with Mary Ann or that Tillis, they're trash and just on temporary," Emma had whispered. "But Jaylene is a good friend to have when trouble comes to visit."

Liberty glanced across the stage. Jaylene was standing in a cross-armed slouch, looking like she'd done everything scandalous once and everything dangerous twice, snapping her fingers to the soft tune Billy Wayne was riffling on the piano.

"Shut up!" Travis yelled, strutting into the tent.

Billy looked at Thomas, who didn't move but one drum stick in a shrug as Travis walked around, swinging a little too close to each of the women for comfort.

"Everybody out of here," Travis shouted suddenly. "Go on. Everybody but you, Emma."

What's this all about? Liberty asked in a glance. Emma shrugged.

Liberty walked through the tent. The grass was yellow and the ground flat enough so the benches sat level. Emma told her that three weeks ago in Florida, one end of the stage sunk nearly six inches into the ground, making it damn hard to tap dance and stay upright at the same time. Liberty felt sorriest for Billy Wayne; wet or dry, soft ground or hard, his piano stool never failed to tilt. In spite of it, he was a damn good piano player. Emma says when we all get a little better we'll ditch Travis and this moth-eaten hunk of canvas and perform indoors for a change. With our luck it'll be a cow barn or the back of a saloon, Liberty thought, stepping into fresh air.

Across the field, she could see a church steeple like a blazing white triangle in the hard Southern sunshine. The man they rented the lot from said the land was donated to the Baptists to build their church on and they built it by faith. Sure, she thought. Mamie used to say that churches that were built by faith means the workers weren't paid enough.

"Hello, Liberty," a voice came softly.

She turned. "Hello, Will."

His face was already red from the heat as he stood there with a sledge hammer in one hand. The only white man traveling with the Revue, he was the cook, the mechanic, and if he absolutely had to he would play his accordion, though every song he touched sounded like a polka. She followed him as he walked around testing the tent's guy ropes.

"Rotting," he said, pulling one.

"Will it hold?"

"Don't know."

"Travis do anything about it?"

His face changed slightly and she knew her answer. He kicked a tent peg, then dropped the hammer on the splintered head. A weak bang of metal striking tired wood and a puff of dust followed. Sort of like a gunshot underground, she thought absently.

He nodded at the horizon. "I don't like the look of them clouds."

"I wish it *would* rain and cool things down."

"Don't wish too hard. A good rain will wash us out of business and into the Gulf of Mexico."

She walked toward the next line.

"Liberty?"

Crossing her arms, she turned to face him.

"I'm sorry about the other day."

She grasped the rope. Tight from rain and use, it seemed to bite into her palm.

"It wasn't the right thing to do."

"It's okay, Will."

And it was still okay, she thought, looking away from Will to the handfuls of snow the wind was throwing at the window. What's not okay is Emma in Alabama. She just had to go there, be in the middle of things. Emma Nevada, always suspicious of crusades and idealism, now busy being a hero. What I would do to know what will happen. Liberty smiled softly. We're all in need of fortune-tellers sometimes, aren't we, Emma? She sipped her beer and set the can on the coffee table.

"Remember the chocolate-covered cherries?" Will said softly.

She stared at the edge of the coffee table, suddenly feeling shy. "How could I forget?"

Will studied the beer can cradled in both of his large hands. "You fallen in love yet, Liberty Grace?"

"Love? Boy, what you saying? That train passed me by years ago."

"That's too bad. Of all the people I know, you should have the good luck to fall in love."

They listened to the wind. Maybe once I would've fallen in love, she thought, watching a sheet of snow slide down the frosted window. No one outside, from what she could see. Only a fool would be outside; only a fool would travel in this weather. She glanced at her hands, palms turned upright to stare at the lines, wishing she could read them.

"Remember how you'd sit up front of the truck and read to me? Let's see, *Tale of Two Cities, The Last of the Mohicans, Native Son.* You know, I never did understand the end of that book. You read it to me over and over. I think about it now and still don't get it." He finished his beer and set the empty can on the coffee table. "And you read me every single newspaper from every little town we stopped in."

"Every part, you said. That was the rule. Headlines, obituaries, wedding announcements—"

Will shut his eyes. " 'Mr. and Mrs. Robert E. Lee Jameson from Winhok, Texas, would like to announce the marriage of their daughter, Geneva, to Richard Mattings Hillbridge, of Macon, Georgia, on May 15, 1952, at the True Believer Episcopal Church. The bride was attended by four bridesmaids, each wearing lovely pale pink linen frocks with seed pearls and French lace collars.' Want me to keep going?"

"Silly, frivolous things written by silly, frivolous people and all we could do is stay out of their way. I've always been nervous around upright citizens."

He opened his eyes. "Me, too. Do you remember when you bought those red shoes, wore them once in two weeks when the left one split up the side? We were in Daisetta and you wanted to drive all the way back to Waco to get your money back. We'd driven over a hundred fifty miles, played Lott, Rosebud, Cameron, Giddings, Greenvine and Hempstead, and all you could think about was going back."

"How do you remember all that stuff?"

"I don't know. I just do. I can recall just about everything I hear. Anyway, we're sitting in Tomball, when Emma shows up with another pair of shoes for you. I have no idea where she got them—"

"—or how much she paid. They were a lot nicer than the first pair. Real calfskin."

He shifted in the chair again, swinging one leg over another so his ankle balanced on top of his knee. "That Emma."

"Don't know what I'd do without her. Go barefoot, I guess."

He smiled and glanced around the room. "You seem to be doing well, Liberty. I'm glad for you."

"I do all right, Will." She nodded, looking at the white ceiling and white walls she had painted, the framed mirror over the mantle making the room look bigger, and hardwood floors with a blue braid rug. It was comfortable and it was hers.

"You dancing again?"

"Teaching. At Anderhazy School of Dance down Lake Street."

"And you do what you want, when you want," he said softly. "But you still haven't fallen in love."

His voice is so sad, could break my heart right out, she thought. Liberty stood up. "Let me show you the rest of my house."

She took him by the hand and led him to her bedroom. His large hands were steady when he reached for her face. I don't love him, she thought, but he is a good man and it has been too long. On the fifteenth of February, she sent him away. Outside, the cab honked for the third time. He picked up his small bag.

"Come with me."

"No," she answered softly.

He watched her for a moment. "I'll keep in touch."

"When you find Emma, tell her to do the same," she said, shivering as she stood by the open door.

Will studied her face as if taking a photograph and left.

The chocolate-covered cherries he had brought her for Valentine's Day lasted till she started bringing pistachio ice cream home by the half-gallon. One Friday, she stopped at a record store to buy "Don't You Just Know It," a new single by Huey "Piano" Smith and the Clowns, and *Sketches of Spain,* to bring her Miles Davis collection up to date, then at the hardware store for two gallons of yellow paint for her bedroom. With the stereo blasting away, she painted the walls while doing the Twist. By April she was sure and called for an appointment. She hummed all the way from the doctor's. Liberty Grace Jones was twenty-nine years old and had a short list of moments when she wanted to dance steps on and off the curb. She wanted to throw something in the air and catch it, she wanted to stand perfectly still on the sidewalk in front of Central High School and laugh. In the daytime, she felt so full of happiness it flicked off her fingertips.

But nighttime and doubts crowded her out of sleep. I know that I am not in love with Will Ross. Love can be rolled into a ball, sent bouncing down a hill and still manage to stick together. This just makes me want to look at people's faces more clearly to see if they know I'm glowing. She sighed. Deep in Liberty's heart, a cold hard kernel had been buried by Mamie. For a moment in the darkness of her own bedroom, shame and disloyalty burned her face.

"Light ones," she could hear Mamie say, her voice cracking from pain, "Light ones like you. Why don't you bleach your skin and be white? Go back to them, then all our enemies will be in one place, not taking food and shelter in our homes."

"Leave me alone, Mamie," Liberty whispered what she was sure had been a shout.

"Sure, sweet thing, I'll leave you alone. Soon as I'm dead. Even then, I'll make it a point to find you." By now, the cancer in her body had blossomed like a rose; the booze she drank for the pain encased her like armor and no one wanted to get close. "Liberty Grace, you looking at me?"

She nodded.

"I can't hear you."

"Yes, I'm looking at you."

"Get over here. Listen to me or I'll slap you so hard, you'll wake up on the other side of life."

Liberty dropped the dirty linen she'd gathered and walked over to the bed.

"I know who you are. And I know what you are. Better than *you'll* ever know." Mamie lay back on the bed. "Now hand me that bottle."

Liberty leaned back against the headboard of her bed. Changing the sheets, repainting the room, nothing would change what had happened here. What I wanted to happen here, she corrected. I brought him to my bed. On the second day, the storm had quit and the sun broke through the clouds and into this room, turning my skin the color of honey.

"You are beautiful, Liberty Grace," Will said, staring up at her sitting above him.

"And I'm going to go snow-blind looking at you." She couldn't stop comparing their colors, seeing his white and pink body as too different, too foreign. Like he brought me pleasure as a gift at an altar and laid it at my feet. And while I stood there trying to figure what to do with it, Mamie came back to tap me on the shoulder, cross her arms and watch. She's come to remind me I'm a traitor, I'm a traitor because of this, she thought, hand on her belly. Porcelana, Vaseline, Jergens lotion, soap, none of them could wash away the stain of disloyalty. I gave up something of myself in those three days. Now this child is mine. A trade. Nothing had changed, but everything, everything is different.

"That's why I resisted," Liberty said to the dark wall across from her, "Even when I didn't." This is my child and my house is good enough for my child. In her mind, she could see snow-covered Banfield Street with her small, black-shuttered house at the end. Not like the house on Rondo, she thought, so cold the heat froze to the windows and the little isinglass window of the hard coal burner gleamed like a peephole to hell.

When she turned thirty on July fifth, more people than her doctor knew of her condition, especially the foul-mouthed sonsabitches who leaned out of their car windows. When I die, she thought, I'm going to hang around to knock over anybody I have a mind to, starting with them. Her weight shifted. She became heavy on her feet and every morning awoke craving food she'd never tasted before. The summer went by in a haze of Coltrane's *Giant Steps,* aches and wonder till September, when she couldn't see her own feet anymore and sleep became a pleasant memory. Let's get this over with, she thought, settling into the recliner. On the end table sat the wooden box, shining in the light of the sunrise. She picked it up and opened the lid. The cobalt cat lay on its back, front paws calmly together. Lifting it out, she held it up to the light. Turns the whole room blue.

Now the world will know…
Even now, after all these years and broken in half, it's a beautiful thing.

"Water's ready, Liberty," Israellen said, as she walked down the hall.

"Thanks, baby," she replied absently. Gently, she placed the cat back, touching the worn spot of velvet in the place where the cat's feet go. Some memories sneak up on little cat's feet, others with as much grace as a freight train. Setting the box back in its place, she glanced around the small room. I don't know, she thought. Earth tones are supposed to make a person feel at ease, but all the browns and tans I got in this room make me feel buried under a pile of dead leaves.

Just what her blues is all about...

Isra waited until Liberty turned off the bath water before pulling the chair out again. First position. *Plié.* Arms graceful. Chin up, up, she could hear Madame say, eyes forward. There is no pain that you feel. And again. Lift. The hands must be perfect—your hands, Israellen, are naturally graceful, but you mustn't count on them to cover your weaknesses, weaknesses like overextension in the back. Isra exhaled. Fifth position front. *Battement retiré,* then *addagio* to *developé.* Straighten that knee. Arch the foot. Damn it. And hands. Hands up. Hands, Madame said, sculpt the air around you. Hands prepare the air to receive you.

Liberty lathered her hands and raised them to her face. This soap smells like a rich man's funeral, she thought. Rinsing off, she looked through the bubble bath at her belly. Yellow, I am almost yellow, especially the stretch marks. I'm almost the color of the winter sun. With one finger, she traced the scar across her middle. When I first saw it, I thought a lumberjack had come after me with a chain saw. She sighed.

Emma Nevada touched her cheek gently that night at the hospital. "Sleep, darling," she whispered.

Her hand is so cool, Liberty thought, closing her eyes. And strong. Useful hands. How many times she tried to grow long nails and failed because she breaks them changing spark plugs or screwing in a hinge.

Emma's hands were still strong, nails long on her right hand and chewed down to the skin on her left. She showed up at the house on Banfield Street two years later with a copy of *Basie at Birdland* in her knapsack and a guitar. The twins were all belly and eyes and odd tucks of shyness and the c-section scar across Liberty's belly wasn't the tearing gap it had first appeared.

"They've grown up beautiful," Emma said the next day, glancing from one to the other.

"Thank you," Liberty said proudly, picking up a building block from the floor and setting it on the end table.

"Think they'll be dancers like their mama?"

"They'll be learning, just like I did."

"Yeah, you'll teach them the same way you taught me: 'Do it Emma, or I'll break your head open.' "

Liberty laughed easily. "I never said that."

"Sure, you did. You just forgot in your amazement at my talent. Now, which is which?"

"This," Liberty said, scooping up the closest to her, "is Israellen. And that is Ricki. You going to tell me what you did to your hair?"

"You like it?"

"Sure, Dandelion Head."

"It's a Natural."

"What happened to grease, press and curl?"

"We're all guilty of running with the pack sometimes, Liberty Grace." Emma picked up Ricki and studied her closely. "She looks white."

"You have a problem with that?" Liberty asked, her voice even.

"No," Emma answered. "But are you sure they didn't get mixed up at the hospital?" With that, she swung Ricki into the air and the little girl giggled. "You like that, huh?" she said, rubbing noses with her.

The twins stayed home with Emma now when Liberty went to work, which was better than dragging them clear across the city on the 21A. Liberty would watch them before she left. Isra was quick, steady and loved to scream. Ricki was clumsy, getting slowly to her feet, but once up she'd run as fast as she could at Emma, who would catch her and flip her in the air. Emma told her that after lunch the twins would fall asleep, Isra on Liberty's recliner and Ricki under the coffee table. Liberty felt a sharp twinge. I miss that. I miss watching them every day, the common things of morning and evening.

Three days after Christmas, Emma and Liberty staggered into the living room at six in the morning to find that one of the girls had turned on the radio, and now the two of them were hopping around the living room with their hair sticking out all over their heads, dancing in their pajamas.

Coffee? Liberty asked Emma with a raised eyebrow. Emma nodded her head and they shuffled into the kitchen.

"Strange kids, Liberty Grace."

"You rubbed off on them."

Emma watched them bobbing on the couch together. "You going to tell me who their daddy is?"

Liberty stared at the new chrome teapot.

"You going to tell them?" Emma asked gently.

Late one night that spring Liberty found Emma leaning over the crib, staring at the twins' faces while they slept. The sweet smell of grass came in through the window, and in the white-blue light from a streetlamp Liberty studied her silhouette.

"What you doing in here, Emma Nevada?" she whispered.

"Watching your babies sleep."

Liberty walked stocking-footed to the end of the bed and stared down. The twins, so different in the light of day, lay curled facing one another, foreheads almost touching and inhaling each other's breath. Gently, Liberty lay her hand on Emma's arm.

"They're all we got in this world, Liberty Grace."

Liberty sighed and leaned her head against her best friend's shoulder. "Yes," she whispered. All we got.

"And we got us," Emma said, curling her arm around Liberty's back and squeezing her very tightly for a moment. Emma left later that morning, only to return with a Freedom Rider on the run from Memphis, fearing for his life because he'd dared to sit in the wrong part of a Greyhound bus from Nashville to Atlanta. He sat in the living room smoking nonstop as if God had set him on fire, his brain so scrambled from fear he could hardly put two words together.

"We had nowhere else to go, Liberty Grace," Emma explained.

"He can stay in the basement."

Two days later when they knew it was safe to move, Liberty packed them chicken salad sandwiches, filled her thermos with coffee, and made Emma take the extra quilt in the linen closet. "If you get stranded, you won't freeze."

"We won't get stranded."

"What if you run out of gas?"

"We won't, Liberty."

Pressing the quilt into her best friend's arms, she looked into Emma's warm eyes.

"I'll return it," Emma said suddenly.

"And it better be clean." Liberty's voice was stern. She swallowed hard, twice, as Emma and the Freedom Rider slipped out the front door and into a waiting truck that drove down Banfield Street in the early morning.

Emma'd come back and go, come back and go, always moving around, Liberty thought. Nothing new in that. Since Emma joined the troupe, off she'd go for days, a week, sometimes more. Some people in the troupe who didn't know any better thought she was shooting smack, but I knew. She was into something bigger, something dangerous, something more addictive than heroin. She was spying for the Movement, sneaking around looking for ways to undermine the white people. Then I moved here and my girls were born. Terry Cee came to live with us after Rita threw him out, stayed till the summer before the twins started school. Then he left, too. All those people going in every direction. Wonder what would've happened to all of us if we'd managed to stay in the same place. Raising her arms, Liberty arched her back to stretch, trying to untie the knots of winter in her muscles.

The blues ain't nothing but a pain in your heart...

Isra reached up. First position. *Plié.* Again. Again. The six basic positions must be internalized by bone and muscle to prevent injury. *Plié.* You cannot afford to be injured because only those with the most perfect bodies will dance ballet. Let your body memorize them, let your muscles learn them as does your mind. She concentrated on seeing the movement, letting memory guide her. Isra's muscles had begun learning on the first day of class.

"They can start ballet tomorrow, but no toe shoes till I say," Liberty had grumbled. "Deforms the feet."

That night on the bus Ricki plopped in her favorite seat, the first one behind the back door, and slumped so her entire body covered it. "What do you call it when somebody thinks she's queen of the dance class?"

"Prima donna," Liberty answered, looking intently out the window. This new class meant it was dark out when they caught the bus for home, and it was hard to be sure where they were on the route.

"That's what you are, Israellen," Ricki accused. "A prima donna."

"I am not," she wailed.

Ricki pushed her fingers into her ears and closed her eyes. "Primadonnaprimadonnaprimadonnaprimadonnaprimadonna," she chanted.

"Ricki! Cut it out!"

"—primadonnaprimadonnaprimadonna—"

"Stop it! Liberty!"

"Hush, Isra," her mother whispered. "The prima donna is the best dancer."

"Really?" she asked hopefully.

42

"Really."

"Ohhh."

Ricki took another breath. "Primadonnaprimadonna-primadonnaprimadonna—"

Isra sat back and looked out the window. She could see the downtown lights over the city reflected in the clouds like a mushroom cap in the sky. Against its haze and the drops of light from Lake Street, she could see her own face reflected in the window. The bus jerked to a stop, doors slapping open to spit out someone, then roared slowly to a start again. The very best dancer, she thought. I am the prima donna.

When you get a bad start…

Prima donna. Balancing on the edge of the chair, Israellen lifted her leg. Higher. Reach. There is no pain in dance, Madame says, just the body trying to say it cannot do what is waiting to be accomplished. Stretch. Isra's face felt hot, like a thin, invisible mask was pressing against her skin. A dull ache surrounded her kneecap. It's what old age feels like, she thought suddenly.

But it will heal. I know it will.

"Israellen!"

"Yes!" she shouted back.

"Would you make me a cup of tea?"

"Sure. Is that what you want for dinner?"

"I think so. When will Ricki be home?"

"I don't know, she didn't say." Isra heard the bath water go on again. She smiled and reached for the battered old tea kettle. Liberty's going to wrinkle up one of these days. I can see her going to Parent-Teacher Conferences then; everybody will know why Ricki does so bad at school—her mother is a raisin.

You and your man have to part…

Liberty sighed and turned the bath water off with her foot. I think I live from one bath to another. All the dancing and all the raising children, none of it seems as real as slipping into hot

43

water after a day like this. I think I live in Minnesota just to get that feeling. I feel, I feel, I feel that old feeling coming on, like Soul Brother Number One Mister James Brown says. She sighed again and slipped deeper into the water, letting her arms relax so her hands floated on the surface. What hands. Not graceful like Isra's, certainly, but useful like Emma's, and strong. Strong enough to smooth a path clear in the world for my children, like hands pushing water to leave a low ebb after passing. Long enough for them to get through? I hope so. I certainly hope so.

But I ain't going to just sit around and cry...

There was a light tapping at the door. "Liberty?"

Only Isra knocks, though god knows where she got manners like that. "Come on in, baby."

"Want some tea now?"

"No, thanks, sweetheart. I'll be out in a minute. Where did you say Ricki was?"

"Band practice, I think. She took her guitar."

"I've told her a hundred million times not to take that guitar outside in this cold. Bad for the wood. Damn thing is older than she is—you don't treat a guitar like that. When I was on the road, the instruments got better treatment than the musicians. Wash my back, honey?"

Israellen lathered soap onto her mother's back, scrubbing her shoulder blades till she could see red scratches from her nails lining her mother's honey skin.

This girl has got the magic touch, Liberty decided, shutting her eyes. *Some days I feel like I grow a whole other layer of skin as protection against the day, and every night she scrubs it right off like I was a snake in need of help. Oh, does that feel good.*

And I know I won't die...

Isra rubbed the top of Liberty's back, the hard triangles from the tops of her shoulders to her neck. Sharp ridges of her backbone rose out of Liberty's skin like a mountain lying sideways, the muscles tight as if any moment expecting attack.

Feels like she's got stones in there, Isra decided, wiping off the soap. "How's that?"

"Wonderful. Child, you are a blessing." Liberty inhaled deeply and opened her eyes. "Isra, how hard are you working that knee?"

Israellen folded the washcloth and hung it over the edge of the tub. Her hands stung, dried out from the soap. "No more than usual."

'Cause I love him...

Liberty leaned back against the tub. "Usual is more than you should be doing."

Isra straightened the yellow bath rug with the toe of her shoe then dried her hand on a towel, her skin still stinging. I can take care of myself, Liberty, the thought sparked in her mind. In the mirror above the sink, she could see Liberty's naked body through the melting patches of bubbles. "There's nothing to worry about," Isra said calmly, squirting Jergens lotion onto her hands and spreading it into her skin. Hands make the air ready to receive you. "Really."

"Your leg needs time to heal."

"I know, Liberty."

Walking down the hall back to the living room, Isra imagined the bones in her leg and foot as a picture in an anatomy book she once looked at, now moving together. The only gracelessness centered around that knee and she consciously shortened her stride to catch the hitch. No way am I going to spend the rest of my life a cripple. I will get better, I will heal. I will dance. I will be the prima donna.

Israellen slipped down the path, feet sliding in the fine sand. Dropping her hand to steady herself, a thorn plunged into her skin near the nail of her thumb. Damn, she thought, plucking out the short sticker and putting her thumb in her mouth. Isra glanced up at the round green hills. Who'd think beneath all this color are miles of sand? The salt-iron taste of blood filled her mouth. Blood tastes like the color red. Ice tastes like the color white, and spring can only taste like the color green, almost the same green as these hills around me.

She noticed suddenly that the line of the mountains looked like the profile of a woman lying on her back. Her hairline gave way to a sloping forehead, a small indent where her nose began and a crest for her lips. A curve to her chin and a longer curve of her throat gave way to the soft rise of her breasts. The edge of the circling mountains traveled halfway around the beach as her stomach till her hipbones rose and fell to her thighs and her knees. Her shins angled sharply down and her feet were ankle-deep in surf.

Israellen could feel sadness coming up from the sand. Even a single white star seemed to shine a thin ray of mourning from the evening sky. I could cry here. "Weep? I have no more tears. I must throw my body upon the earth so it may mourn silently." Hecuba in *The Trojan Women*. How I hate that play, I hate it so much some of the lines stick to me. But how good it will feel to lie in the sand and let all the brooding leave me. To let all this and Caleb go.

It was almost an afterthought, this anger at Caleb, a dividend from everything else she felt, forcing her to see clearly, as if anger were a bucket of tears splashed into her eyes. Her fury made her watchful and the more she saw, the angrier she became till Israellen was sure she had a two-edged glance. If looks could kill, Caleb Duncan would be dead on the kitchen floor and the murder weapon sheathed under long lashes. "You had to pick now, didn't you?"

"No time like the present." He finished the whiskey and poured another. "I'm sure your sister will understand."

"Who cares if my sister understands? I don't."

"It was a joke. Sex is always a joke."

You bastard. He says it as if what we have is a joke, too, nothing to be concerned or to rejoice about. She glanced back at the woman in the mountains. How am I to react when I find him in my bed with someone else on the day Ricki shows up? Why would he say that Ricki would understand—what does she have to do with us? Why did he do it? Why does he act like he doesn't care? Because he doesn't. I wonder if he ever did. I thought we were happy. I thought he loved me. I thought I loved him, but love can't fill in what's mismatched or broken.

She studied the outline of the cliff. The woman lying on her back sleeps while the stars are happy just watching. The moon wants to hold her but can't get close, so it sends the tide in its place. The waves splash against the rocks like a thousand hands reaching for her, every blast weakening the cliffs that hold her up to the sky. Maybe the ocean is secretly jealous. Maybe the ocean wants her, too.

Two

Ricki shoved the extra sweatshirts into the bag and hefted it to her shoulder. Been so long since I've had plans of my own, she thought, starting down the path to the sea. Been so long since I've been living my own life, not the life people are waiting to see onstage. Some people say they get lost when they're playing. Not me. Not at all. I'm always here, only the place changes. Everyday life is like clothes folded up in my suitcase. The money, the girlfriends, the travel, I take them off and hang them in a closet, so when I play, those things aren't here, they're not what I'm playing. When I play, it's like getting on a subway, riding one long train and not till two miles and twenty stops go by do I realize that I'm moving, that I started back at one end and I'm heading for the other. Between here and there, I've been playing but people listening can only hear me at the stops.

I keep returning to the memories. Thinking about the smell of my neighborhood, my favorite shirt when I was nine, sixteen, twenty. So many pieces of taste and sound, a lifetime of them, but only a minute on the clock goes by. A minute on the clock gives me enough. I can write and play one memory forever by the clock. The greats do. They take a moment and let it ripple through everything, till that single memory takes up the whole room and people get covered with it. All the living in an arpeggio. All that sensation in a triplet, variations in unexpected registers. Imagine how fast I could live, how much I could do if time on the clock, that military march of tick-tock could be bent like a string on my guitar. I got a hundred lives to live; I got all those who came before me and before them and before them.

Pretty country, smoky and green, love the way the mountains look so soft, different from the Rockies, that's for sure. I'll have to come back here someday. Seems like my kind of place. Quiet. Private. A place where people will leave me alone. Place where I could stand on any of these hills and sing my heart out to the sky if I was so inclined. Everybody needs a place like this.

Liberty'd been right; Queenie the turtle made it to the middle of October and croaked off. There wasn't much else to do with her now, except dig a small pit at the end of the garden where the dirt was loose, put the shoebox that held what was left of the turtle in it, and try explaining death to her eight-year-olds. Isra patted the small mound softly with her hand as Liberty leaned on the shovel.

"Shouldn't we say something?" Isra asked.

"Say what you think best," Liberty replied.

"When me and Rickshaw have funerals, she always says something religious, then we sing."

Where was Ricki anyway? "Get on with it."

"What should I say?" Isra looked up at her mother.

She is a beautiful child, Liberty realized. "Just say whatever comes into your head, sweetie."

"You do it."

Liberty sighed. "Goodbye, Queenie. You were a good friend."

"And a good turtle."

They both stared at the little hump of dirt.

"We should sing now," Isra said solemnly.

They got through the first line of "Amazing Grace," which was as far as Liberty planned to go, when Ricki's voice sailed over them. Liberty looked around the small yard, but still couldn't find her. "Where is she?"

Isra stood up and pointed.

"Rickshaw Jones," Liberty shouted to her. "Get the hell off that roof."

Ricki walked back and forth, arms out like a tightrope walker. *"I once was lost—"*

"Rickshaw!"

"— but now am found—"

"I said get down. Now!"

" 'Twas blind—"

"Rickshaw! Dammit!"

Isra's eyes went wide. "You shouldn't swear at a funeral, Liberty."

" —but now I see." Ricki stopped, standing on the edge of the roof near the rain gutter. "The end."

"Get off there, right now."

"Want me to go and get her?" Isra asked.

"Shut up, Isra."

"Just trying to help, geez," she said, crossing her arms.

"Get down, Rickshaw."

"Why? I ain't going to hurt myself. We been up here zillions of times. Besides, Queenie's spirit has to get to the other side. How she going to do it if God doesn't hear me?" She took a deep breath and opened her arms to the sky and started singing. *"Deep River, Lord / My home is over Jordan —"*

"What song is that?" Liberty asked, amazed.

"It's a gospel song."

"We don't have any gospel records."

"Deep River, Lord—"

"She learned it at the library. She heard it in one of their little rooms. They won't let you take anything out unless you have a grown-up library card." Isra shoved the toe of her shoe into the dirt that covered Queenie.

"I want to cross over—"

"Ricki always climbs to the highest place to sing, we even

53

once climbed the water tower by school. She says because we're kids and since there's so many people praying, we got to take all the advantages we can. She says if God hears us, then whatever we pray for will come true."

"—into Canaan—"

"How did she learn all this about God?"

"I told you: records at the library. She listens to all of them in a little room with carpet on the walls. She listens to all the good ones like Mahalia and Aretha."

"Aretha."

"Deep River, Lord—"

"And Miss Bessie, but there aren't many of those, and somebody named Charlie Christian. He plays guitar. We get to wear headphones."

"You don't learn about God from a record."

"Ricki did. She says she can hear God talking in the gospel choirs."

"Hey," Rickshaw shouted suddenly. "Quit talking about me."

At the end of the gravel path, Ricki stretched her neck and took a deep breath. The salt seemed to sink from the air to her lungs and all the way to her bones. Maybe I'll ride a motorcycle through here when the tour is over, maybe bring Yaz and the boys through here, jam in those funky little pubs they got, just for the fun of it. Like old times. She grinned as she trudged through the sand. Old days, damn, I'm twenty-five years old, what do I know about old days? I sound more like Yaz every day. Maybe I should live near the ocean when I get back to America. Just the smell of the ocean makes everything seem alive, it's so different from the big dirty cities like Chicago and New York and Atlanta.

The band was late getting to Isra's. The cab had gotten hung up in traffic and by the time they pulled up to Isra and Caleb's flat, Yaz was asleep and drooling on the car door, Malcolm and Marcel were snoring and Ricki's eyes were burning. Wish I could fall asleep. Funny how I want to fall asleep during all the long moments. I don't mind the bad shit between people, I can handle consequences and disasters, but hell, this waiting business just seems to scratch and scratch till my skin's gone and my nerves are laying open for anything to attack them. I've got one day with Isra till the tour is over. One day to get over jet lag, one day to say hello. Just enough time to meet Caleb and get some sleep. Four years, four years I haven't seen her and all I have is time to say hello. Jesus Christ, what has happened to me when I can't even spend time with my baby sister, when I'm hoping and fearing she will want to see me at all? Ricki dragged her band up the stairs and pounded on the small door.

It swung open.

"Hello, Israellen," Ricki said quietly.

"Hello, Rickshaw."

"You remember Malcolm, Marcel and Hezekiah, don't you?"

"Do I smell breakfast?" Yaz asked, suddenly awake.

Isra's smile was perfect. "Yes. Come in, all of you."

The door closed behind them as they filed into the living room.

Ricki glanced around the flat. "Where's your husband?"

"He's on location in Scotland for the rest of the week."

"Working on a movie?"

"A commercial. I miss him, of course."

Yaz blew out a lungful of Lucky Strikes smoke in their faces. "When do we eat?"

"Right now. Help yourselves." Isra turned to her sister. "You're staying here with me, aren't you, Ricki? You'll have to sleep in my bed, but that'll be okay, won't it?"

"Shit," Yaz grumbled. "I'm the talented one, let me sleep with you."

Ricki searched the path ahead of her. Isra wasn't in sight. Might already be at the beach, wonder how far away it is?

55

Siobhan said it was a nice walk, not too far and considering how lazy she is, I know it's got to be around the bend or over the hill. Siobhan would just as soon lay in bed all day, not that I could really protest, seeing as how I'd join her if I could. Wonder if she'd consider going back to the United States with me.

Siobhan was a small woman—Ricki could scoop her up as easy as a Sunday paper—and when she introduced her to the band, one of the guys, she was sure it was Yaz, wolf-whistled. She was beautiful and had a sharp spark of humor that made Ricki laugh often and easily. Plus she had the most wonderful skin Ricki had ever touched. A fine deep color that darkened from her hips to her ankles.

"What's the matter, haven't you ever heard of black Irish before?" she had sassed at Ricki the first time they met at the Black Cap. Should've known she was Irish, Ricki thought. She drinks like sand and talks nonstop. Siobhan's skin was so soft, she wondered how she'd escaped the trouble of living every-day to keep such skin. She had no calluses, she's not a woman used to hard labor or walking far, Ricki realized. Mornings Ricki'd wake up early just to look as she slept. Almond eyes, arching brows, the sure curves of her body welcoming to touch—why didn't we gig over here before and give me the chance to meet her sooner?

The contract the band signed included two hotel rooms with kitchens. If there was one thing Ricki couldn't stand it was being without the chance to cook. She even brought her favorite paring knife, which made the airport scanner beep when she walked through. She cooked because she liked to and because she was good at it. Siobhan had mastered the art of making instant coffee.

"Morning, love," Siobhan said softly, the small scar near her eye turning into a star as she smiled. She straddled Ricki's thighs.

Sweetness, Ricki thought, breathing the scent of her. She pushed her face against Siobhan's breasts. "Good morning."

"Why don't you be a darling and cook something for me. Cheese on toast and tomatoes."

"Toe-may-toes."

"Toe-maw-toes."

"Say it right or go hungry."

"Yanks."

Siobhan was splashing in the bathtub when the hot plate fell. Ricki caught it and by the time she set it on the counter, the tops of the fingers on her left hand were a blazing red. Her throat went tight, but not as tight as the grip she had on her left wrist to stop the pain from going any further. She turned on the cold water and shoved her hand into it, her body starting to shake as the white bubbling stream cooled the burns. Sweat seeped out on her forehead and stung her scalp. Christ. She pulled her hand out of the water, still gripping her wrist and looked. Red. And angry-looking and feeling like a thousand ants were trying eat their way out of her skin.

"Ricki?" Siobhan asked, coming into the kitchen wearing only water from the tub. "What's wrong?"

"Nothing." Ricki shoved her hand back into the water. Even out for a peek started it to stinging.

"What did you do to yourself?"

"It's all right. Go and eat." How in the hell was she going to play tonight?

"Rick—"

"For god's sake, leave me alone." She spun away from the sink, guarding her hand. There had to be something that would help. Butter might. That's what Liberty used. Ricki stretched her fingers. Little white blisters were forming under the skin. Hell, hell, hell. Like somebody's using my hand as a pin cushion, sticking needles with pieces of thread still on the end like miniature battle flags. Pins and needles, pins and needles, that's what Liberty called the funny feeling you get when your leg's asleep, she remembered. The tops of her ears felt wind-burned and she was suddenly dizzy. Pins and needles.

*   *   *

Ricki tightened her hand into a fist as she walked the gravel path towards the beach. It was hell those first few nights. Like Isra, with her leg. Work it out, forget the pain, because it's all you got to believe in. She stretched her long legs, taking larger steps. The muscles in the backs of her thighs thrummed, feeling almost as if they were too short for her legs. All the sitting, she thought. Drinking beer and playing the blues every night, riding from town to town, my legs must be shrinking from no exercise. Legs are a funny part of the body. I never worry about my legs, never worry about not walking, not being able to move or tap my feet to music, but when they ache, they really ache. And when legs get hurt, they really get hurt.

"Something broke in her knee when she fell, too."

"Jesus, Liberty, how did it happen?"

"Don't know. Madame said her leg just crumpled beneath her."

"Do you want me to come down there?"

"We'll probably be on our way home by the time you do— buses run so strange this time of night."

"I could borrow Rebecca's car."

"I thought you didn't like Rebecca."

"I don't."

"Besides, you don't have a driver's license."

"So?"

"Look, honey, she's been in for awhile, I'm sure we'll be leaving soon. I got to go, there's the doctor. Love."

"Love," Ricki answered automatically. Liberty always said love before she hung up, like sending a letter or something. Ricki glanced around the kitchen. Dinner's ready in the oven— lasagne and garlic bread. I was going to wait till Liberty and Isra were asleep but maybe I don't have to. Bet I have time for Miss Bessie's party, it'll only take a few minutes. "What do you think, Tina Turner?"

The cat was curled like the Sphinx on the stove, watching

the white bakery bag on the counter next to the refrigerator. Inside was a chocolate cupcake with double fudge frosting.

"Don't even think of it, cat," Ricki threatened. Tina Turner's eyes flickered from her to the cupcake as she set it on a plate then stuck a red birthday candle in it. Good color, Ricki thought. Miss Bessie liked red.

Turning off the radio and the kitchen light, she could see through the open window a single star pulsing like a hot white spark. The sky, she decided, is the color of my eyes, as if I looked at it for so long it decided to fill me up. Putting the cupcake on the table, she sat down and lit the candle with her Zippo. The cat leapt up on the table, sitting next to Ricki's hand with her tail curled neatly around her feet. She was still staring at the cupcake.

"We have to wait, Tina Turner," Ricki whispered. The cat glanced at her again, her eyes a deep gold and the small white spot on her face a bright flash against her dark gray fur. Ricki looked around the dark kitchen. The white paint of the cupboards had lines from the brushes they used to remodel the kitchen last spring; now the candle glow seemed to shine up and down in them as if they were trenches for the light. The aluminum trim along the countertops gleamed dully and the burn mark on the wall above the stove looked black, not brown, and like a twisted face in the paint. I could put on one of her records and blast it until Isra and Liberty get home, she thought, suddenly aware that she was listening to nothing but her own breathing and the purring of the cat. I wonder if she listens to herself. I bet you listen to yourself all the time, Miss Bessie. The World's Greatest Blues Singer Will Never Stop Singing, like it says on your gravestone. I got a picture I cut out of the paper. It's in my wallet, behind the part where the dollar bills go.

"Wait, I forgot." She jumped up and opened the cupboard under the sink. Unscrewing the lid from a bottle of gin, she splashed some into two glasses and returned the bottle to its hiding place. Ricki picked up her glass and lifted it in salute at the stars she could see through the kitchen window. Nobody can even get close to how much I love you, Miss Bessie. I love you enough to fill both of us.

"It's September ninth, 1978, Miss Bessie Smith, anniversary of the day you died, the only date I got. I listen to your records, I got a picture of you hanging on my wall. Please come to your party." Ricki squeezed her eyes shut. Bessie, she thought, holding her breath and trying to push the name out of her mind and into the night sky. Please? Ricki breathed out and slowly opened her eyes. Staring at the burning candle, her stomach started to tighten. She felt an almost electric touch on her back, causing the small hairs on her neck to stand up. She's here, Ricki thought. Bessie's come to the party.

A breeze shook the flame of the candle, and it roared in its effort to stay lit. This wind's got an edge on it, Ricki noticed. Indian summer's come, but soon the leaves will turn and the cold will come along to freeze me to nothing. You ever feel like nothing, Bessie? Like the fire of a candle that's been blown out? That's how I feel, sometimes. Like my nerve endings are all wrapped up in cotton and taped so tight, they wouldn't budge during an earthquake.

Another breeze blew the candle out.

"Just like that, Bessie," Ricki whispered, lifting both glasses and clinking them together in a toast. Taking out the birthday candle she unwrapped the cupcake, licking off a hunk of frosting that smeared across her hand. "Come here, Tina Turner," she said, dropping a chunk of cake onto the table for her.

Outside, a scrap of paper rushed across the yard like a bird with broken wings. Look at that, even the trash feels strange, Ricki thought. Paper thinks it can fly tonight. She covered her face with her hands. They smelled like fine wood polish, steel and sweat. Calluses on her fingertips, short nails and a curving scratch from when she and Tina Turner were playing yesterday. Holding them up to silhouette against the sky, she stared at her long fingers. Strong enough to bend steel into any note I want.

"But if I just knew what I want," she said aloud, drinking

the gin from her glass. Yaz says I shouldn't think of playing the blues, should be feeling them, but how can you do that when your nerves are signed, sealed and delivered? Christ, I'm quoting Stevie Wonder to Bessie Smith. She shook her head. The blues, Yaz says, are the human condition. And I'm human, ain't I? Just because I don't look like a sister doesn't mean anything. I am a sister. Not looking like it doesn't mean I'm not. Outside, the piece of paper fluttered again. Trying to show it's not necessarily what it appears to be. Just like me.

Ricki jumped when she heard a car horn honk out front. She dropped the cat onto the floor, swept the crumbs off the table onto the plate and dropped it in the sink, followed by the two glasses. She flicked on the light. Okay. Everything's back to normal. She took a deep breath, hoping Liberty wouldn't catch that she'd been drinking her gin. Liberty won't notice if you don't do anything stupid.

It was stupid, so stupid but it happened, Isra thought, balancing unsteadily on her crutches as the cab pulled away. How can I dance with this thing? she wondered, staring at the cast again, as if she thought staring long enough would make it melt off her leg and disappear into a crack in the sidewalk.

"How long did the doctor say I have to wear this thing?"

"In six weeks we go back for x-rays." The dazed look on her daughter's face froze her.

Six weeks. Recital was in ten. Tryouts for the Dance Theater were two weeks after that. I might make it after all.

"I'll get the door," Liberty said, jumping up the steps.

"I might make the auditions," Isra said hopefully, slowly maneuvering up the stairs.

Liberty looked at her, disbelieving. She didn't hear anything that the doctor said. "We'll see, prima donna. You got to let that leg heal first."

I could keep stretching out, Isra thought, getting through the door sideways and hopping into the living room. Keep working, keep in shape, that should help, and when the cast comes off, I'll only have to work this leg.

"Hey, prima donna," Ricki said, buttoning up a flannel shirt over her tank top and walking in from the kitchen. "You hungry?"

Liberty dropped her purse next to the chair and helped Isra onto the couch. She's all sweat and trembling, she thought, helping Isra with her sweater before taking off her own coat and laying them on the recliner. Liberty propped Isra's leg up with a cushion.

"You keep it up like that, you won't strain it."

"I cooked, even though it was your turn. Gourmet stuff. You'll love it. The lasagne has raisins and wine in it; I just created the recipe." Ricki dashed into the kitchen and returned, balancing three plates. "Ta da," she sang out, setting the plates on the coffee table and pulling out forks from her back pocket.

"Looks good, Ricki," Liberty said, taking hers and sitting in the recliner.

Isra shrugged. "I'm not hungry."

"You should eat anyway, keep your strength up, baby sister. What did the doctor say?"

"Cast comes off in six weeks," Isra stuck in.

"Then you're cured? That's great."

"Then we go for x-rays."

"That's not so great."

"And maybe an operation," Liberty finished, taking a bite of lasagne.

"That sucks. What about tryouts?"

Isra set her plate back on the table, feeling like she was going to puke. "Liberty? You have those pills?"

"Sure," she answered, setting her plate down and searching her purse.

"You okay?" Ricki asked.

"Just aches a little."

"Drugs will help, trust me. Let me see those."

Isra handed the prescription bottle over.

"Greenies. Huh. You sure you want to use these? We could sell them and make a mint."

"Ricki, if I catch you—" Liberty began.

"And deprive prima donna of any relief from pain and agony? Would I do that?"

"Your smarting off would do you a lot more good if you applied it to your school work."

"But I can't," she said, tossing the bottle back to Isra. "I am incorrigible. Want a beer?"

Tina Turner sniffed at Isra's abandoned plate.

"She's eyeing that garlic bread," Liberty observed.

"She can have it," Isra answered.

"I'll give her some more cat food instead," Ricki volunteered, picking up Isra's plate. "Come on, Tina, you pig."

"That kid, I swear." Liberty picked up the other plates and followed her daughter into the kitchen.

"Okay," Ricki whispered, "how bad?"

Liberty shook her head.

"Shit," Ricki hissed.

"Go on back out there and give me that beer," Liberty said quietly, scraping the last of the dinner into the garbage can. My poor girl. My poor little dancer. What are we going to do now? We'll think of something. We always think of something. Emma Nevada, any suggestions you'd care to make would be grand.

"Liberty, do you think we could put a barre up in here so I can stretch out?" Isra asked as her mother walked into the room.

"I don't think you should strain that leg, hon," she answered softly.

"But the audition is two months away."

"There'll be other auditions, Isra," Ricki put in quickly.

Isra shook her head, her face beginning to look pinched around her eyes and mouth. They don't understand. She swung her leg around and slowly stood up. "I'm going to bed."

Isra skipped school the next day because of her leg, so Ricki skipped to keep her company. She tried to show Israellen how to blow smoke rings, how to play guitar and how to roll a joint, but Isra just lay on the couch in the living room with a cushion under her leg listening to her stack of pop albums. Ricki retreated to her own room. She plugged her guitar into her amp and blasted away. Band practice tonight with the punk rock band. She liked playing the music, all the jumping around and attitude, but she wasn't so sure about the other musicians—four white boys with their dirty torn clothes and greasy hair. Ricki let her own hair grow long, though a year ago it was short enough so with half a can of Isra's Aqua Net, she could comb it into a pompadour. Year ago my hair was hip. A year ago I was looking good.

Sort of like Billie Holiday's, she'd thought, giving her hair a last pat before school.

"Look at Rickshaw," Tony said during Remedial Reading, "trying to look like Elvis. Hey, boy, why don't you sing something?"

"That's enough," Mr. Kawazaski, the white teacher said, not even bothering to look up from the attendance list.

"*You smell like a hound dog,*" sang Tony. "Come on, Elvis Junior, sing along with me."

"He needs his guitar," Sandy said. She was a white girl who could crack her gum so loud it sounded like a pistol shot.

"No, he don't. Come on, Elvis," Tony urged, kneeling up in his seat so he towered over Ricki in the desk ahead of him.

Ricki didn't move.

"Hey. Hey, white boy—"

"Shut up!" She turned in her seat, fists clenched.

"I said that's enough!" Kawazaski yelled from the front of the room.

The room was silent for a moment as Ricki stared at Tony.

"What you think you can do to me, bitch?" Tony whispered. "Huh?"

In his eyes she saw a flicker. He loves this shit, she realized. He loves it. She faced front again, concentrating on loosening her fingers.

"What you going to do?" he said a little louder.

"Shut up, Johnson," the teacher called.

"Yes sir, Mr. K," Tony said.

Ricki could feel him sliding back into his chair and immediately began kicking her seat. She shut her eyes for a moment, then slowly opened them. Get a grip, she thought, he can't hurt you unless you let him. Just one more year of this and I am done. Don't let them get to you, don't get thrown out over this asshole dog. That night she washed out the hairspray and left her hair to grow. With a little grease and persuasion, by September she had short dreadlocks.

Ricki leaned against the bedroom wall. Now my hair's to my collar and they hate it. Isra and Liberty can't stand my hair. Wonder if they can even stand me. Jesus, why even think about that stuff? She glanced out the window. The sky was pink; the sun had just set. I'd feel sorry for Isra if she hadn't copped such an attitude, Ricki thought, picking up her guitar and tossing off a few rock chops. Glancing at her hands, she noticed the nail on her left pinkie getting a little long. She gnawed it off. Can't stand having my nails too long. Feels like somebody's scraping my finger bone with a piece of sandpaper when I'm trying to play. Sounds like it too, though that's how punk is supposed to sound. What am I doing playing punk music anyway? Ricki shook her head and riffed through two octaves.

Nineteen fifty-seven Fender Stratocaster. Practically plays itself. Beautiful thing, how could I ever replace you? Ricki gently touched the long scrape on the topside of the neck, from the fourth to sixth fret. Terry Cee did that, she remembered. It's not as bad as the one on the back, made from someone wearing a belt buckle and scraping a square inch of cherry-red finish away. Billy Wayne, maybe Big Henry, when they were all over here jamming one of those nights. And the triangular dent near the tone and volume knobs, below the pickguard. That one was my fault. The guitar fell right out of my arms and smacked the corner of the big old Gibson amp he had.

*　　　　*　　　　*

"Hi, there," Terry Cee said.

"Hi."

"I put you to bed an hour ago. How come you're not sleeping?"

"Isra is sleeping, not me."

He laughed at that. Scooping her up, he balanced her on one knee and his guitar on the other.

"Looks like you got yourself a new girlfriend, baby," his mother Rita cackled from where she sat at the kitchen table.

"Just be sure she don't headlock you into marriage, son," Billy Wayne joked.

Both skunk drunk, Liberty thought. Their reunion won't last more than three days at this rate. "Ricki, honey, you leave Terry Cee alone."

"Can I play?" Ricki asked him instead.

Terry gave her a squeeze. "You going to play guitar when you grow up, aren't you, sweetheart?"

"I want to play now," she said, as seriously as a four-year-old could.

They all laughed. He does love that girl, Liberty thought. One of the best things that happened to all of us was him moving in here after Emma left. Hard to believe a fourteen-year-old boy could behave better than men two, three, five times his age. Taking care of my children, couldn't ask for a better big brother in the world. And quiet, that boy is so quiet, sometimes feels like he isn't really here at all, more like a spirit that makes a body reappear when we want to see him and the rest of the time wafts around my house like a friendly breeze.

"Give the girl a chance, Terry," Henry called from the couch.

"Ricki, you leave him alone," her mother said.

Rickshaw stared at the guitar instead. "Pretty."

"Ain't it?" Terry whispered, setting her down. "Now you hop up there on the amp."

She climbed onto it, her little feet swinging six inches from the floor.

"Hold out your arms." Gently, as if handing her a newborn, he set the Strat onto her lap. "Got it?"

She nodded.

"You sure? It's heavy."

She nodded again.

Terry let go.

Ricki hugged the beautiful guitar. He never let her hold it before, though once she and Isra snuck into his room and played one strum each.

"Give us some music, baby," Billy Wayne said as he got up from his chair and limped over to the portable organ.

"Go ahead, Ricki," Terry urged. "Just run your hands over the strings."

Ricki lifted her right hand, strummed once, and everyone laughed. Terry Cee grinned at her blasting away on his electric guitar. She gave him a great big smile just as it fell.

The body of the guitar landed against the metal corner of the amp and crashed out an ugly sound. Terry grabbed the Strat by the neck and muffled the jangling strings. She watched him turn the guitar over and set it on his lap. With one finger, he traced the edges of the gouge from where it hit.

"Everything okay, son?" Billy Wayne asked.

"Of course it's okay," Rita shouted as she got unsteadily to her feet. "Now play my favorite song, Billy Wayne."

"Hush, woman." Billy was still watching Terry.

"It's okay, Daddy," Terry said suddenly, pulling the guitar upright.

Ricki noticed how worn his black shoes were; they were all she could look at. His socks had slid down into his shoes and let a slice of his calves show from beneath his pants and the hairs were like little black spots on his legs.

"Ricki?"

Her mother's voice shattered her staring.

"You come over here, baby."

Marvin started a slow, smoky bass soon joined with the fat

notes of the organ. Thomas picked up the downbeat, his high hat a bright shimmering sound in the living room. Ricki hopped off the amp to land on her behind in front of Terry. He looked down at her; she stared up at him. Gently, he reached over his guitar and lifted her to her feet.

"I'm sorry," she said softly, a tiny tear at the corner of her eye.

"I know you are. Now, don't start crying, I can't handle women who cry and aren't you my very favorite girl?"

She sniffed and rubbed the back of her hand over her eyes. Her chest felt tight, as if a huge rubber band was wrapped around her, making it hard to breathe.

"Go sit with Liberty. My guitar is all right, it still plays and that's what counts."

Cradling Ricki in her arms, Liberty watched Billy Wayne's fingers moving over the keys. In the soft light of the table lamps, his gold rings gleamed hypnotic as he hip-hopped up and down the keyboard.

Liberty glanced at Rita standing next to him, hand on his shoulder. Some women can turn a boy into a man, she realized.

Blues, why do you worry me...

And some women can turn a man into a boy. Rita's one of those. Liberty glanced at Terry. He played softly, picking his notes carefully, as if playing for his mother was like walking on a mine field as Rita eased through the first verse.

Why do you stay so long...

She's trying very hard to sound like Sassy Vaughan that night we heard her down at the Key Club, Liberty decided. She doesn't even have that kind of voice, what's left of it after the booze and those drugs.

Blues, why do you worry me...

But Terry's good, all those notes float out of that guitar like water. They're all pretty good for amateurs, except Henry, who only brings his trumpet as a charade. But Terry Cee's already better than they are and he's only fourteen years old.

Why do you stay so long…

Liberty leaned back in her chair and touched Ricki's hair. There were bits of fuzz caught in it. Not that she'd ever notice, Liberty thought wryly. She's too busy watching that guitar. Always watching guitars, this girl's been bit by the music bug bad.

Ricki ran a short series of arpeggios into Terry Cee's signature chord progression, then touched the indentation again. Not as bad as it first looked—at first it looked big enough for Terry to throw me in if he wanted. But he retouched it so it's hidden unless you're looking for it. And he never held it against me, even gave me a toy Casper the Friendly Ghost guitar for my next birthday. That was after he moved away and we had to go to the dance school with Liberty every day. I hated that place. Shuffle, step, shuffle, step, ball turn, heel, toe, heel, toe, shuffle, step. I still hate it.

Ricki wrapped the Stratocaster in its plaid blanket and set it gently in its case. Going to have to fix this case, she realized, trying to restick a hunk of duct tape with all the stick gone. It's more tape than case right now; hell, it was falling apart when Terry still had it.

"Did you bring your guitar?"

Terry, seventeen and still clumsy, had barely uncurled himself from behind the wheel of his beat-up Mercury before Ricki started hopping up and down in the driveway. "Don't I even get a hello from my best girl?"

Ricki stuck her hand out. "Slap me five and that's no jive."

Terry laughed. "Come here," he said, pulling her into a hug.

"Where's your guitar?" she asked as soon as he set her down.

"Where's your mama?"

"I asked first."

"I asked second and I'm bigger than you."

"Her and Isra are walking back from the store. I ran."

"You ran to see me?"

"It's not that far." Taking him by the hand, she led him to the cement steps to the front door and sat down. "Where is it?"

He sat next to her. "How do you know I don't have it?"

"Because I looked."

"Could be in the trunk."

"Trunk don't work."

"Maybe I fixed it."

"Terry Cee," Liberty called from the end of the driveway.

"Hi." He got up and walked down the driveway to meet them. "Hey, Isra, how you doing, baby?"

"I'm okay," she answered, struggling with her bag.

"I got it," Terry said, lifting it out of her arms.

Liberty shifted the bag of groceries. "How are you this fine day?"

"Pretty good, pretty good."

"You're right on time. I'm not used to you being here exactly at two o'clock. You must be growing up or something."

"Never," he laughed as they walked in the front door.

"You two," Liberty called to the twins, "stay outside. We'll be leaving in a minute."

"But—"

"No buts, Israellen. Now outside and stay nearby. We're leaving soon. Terry's got other things to do. And don't—"

The screen door slammed.

"—slam the door. Kids!"

They walked to the kitchen and set the bags down. Liberty turned on the small radio on the table. Smokey and the Miracles began easing their way around the room with "Ooh, Baby, Baby" as they unloaded the groceries.

Liberty set the milk and the oranges in the refrigerator then pulled out the bread and grape jelly. My kids eat this stuff like their lives depend on it, she thought. "You hungry?"

"Naw." Terry folded up the empty bag and stuffed it in a small cupboard.

"You sure?" she asked, gesturing with the jelly jar.

"I'm sure. Besides, I will never eat grape jelly for the rest of my life after living in this house." He sat down at the kitchen table.

Liberty smiled and folded the last bag. "You want something to drink?"

He shook his head. "Do you like Smokey Robinson?"

"He's all right. Do you?"

Terry shook his head again. "He sounds like a fag."

She was stung by the hate in his voice. No matter how hard someone tries, she thought, sitting at the table with a can of pop, the bigots always get to the kids first.

"You mind if I turn that off?"

"Go ahead." She sipped the pop. I can feel my teeth rotting already. "How's the band?"

He shrugged. "How's any band?"

"It was fine last Tuesday."

Shrugging again, he scooted a bread crumb across the table with the flick of one finger.

Liberty pushed the pop away from her and leaned back in her chair. Outside, the twins raced around the garage, then raced back out. Playing one of their games again, she decided. She glanced at Terry again. How in the hell motor-mouth Billy Wayne and Rita the Screamer ever made such a quiet child is beyond me.

"I was thinking," he began.

"Yes?"

Terry shifted in his chair. "Maybe I'm going to get my high school diploma."

"Really?" Liberty was surprised.

"I been listening to some of the brothers around town, you know, just listening. Maybe I could go to college, help the people, you know? It's just a dream, I mean, who knows what'll happen. I might get drafted."

"If you do, you let me know and we'll smuggle you into Canada." Liberty sat back in her chair. Vietnam. Something very sick about it. Maybe all those generals ought to rot in the jungle for awhile and see if they like it. "Is college what you want, baby?"

He leaned his head on his hand and played with the bread crumb again. "I don't know. Better than the Army."

"Well, I think I like this idea. I didn't even know you'd been considering it."

"Just recent. Like I said, I been listening to some people, doing some thinking."

"You could talk to Emma about this, she knows lots of college people."

"Maybe. Yeah." He stood up slowly. "Better get going, huh?"

Liberty got out of her chair and picked up her purse. "We have to stop at Henry's house after Anderhazy's. I told Emma we'd pick her up."

Liberty watched Emma crawl into the backseat of Terry's Mercury. "Didn't go so well with Henry?"

"Take a guess." Emma sat in back with the twins, staring out the window as Rondo slid past. The street had been widened since they lived there, the old houses, paint peeling and porches held up with cinder blocks, now reached right up to the road. Groups of people, drinking beer, standing or sitting in the shade of the screened-in porches, listened to music from radios and record players and watched cars crawl down the street in the hot summer sun.

All these people. I don't know any of them anymore, Liberty thought. I used to know the names of every neighbor, knew what they did and how they were related and they sure as hell knew us. The only one who would talk to me other than the Nevadas was Old Annie. Who wanted to talk to her, anyway? A white woman the boys pelted with snowballs in the winter and crab apples in the summer. We always knew she was coming because the baby carriage she used to hold the junk she collected would let out a screech like a nail being pulled from a board. Old Annie never worked; before the war Mamie was always losing *her* job for rabble-rousing. Till Tiger Samuels came by one evening looking for her.

"I understand you had a misfortune here," the thin, well-dressed man said through the screen door.

"Why, yes," Liberty answered in her best adult voice. "We do. We have a Miss Mamie Fortune."

And Mamie started working at Tiger's—"If We Can't Fix It, It Isn't Broke" was his motto. He knew Mamie was a fine worker, could fix about anything and could rabble-rouse all she wanted since she'd be the only one in the shop. He was busy courting Lila May Adair, of the funeral parlor Adairs, and always looking at himself in windows and chrome bumpers to slick his hair back. Tiger's shop was a whitewashed shack exactly 268 steps from our house and when I was just a little thing, I thought that was good luck—it was almost the same number as our house, 628 Rondo.

As the Mercury drove past, Liberty saw a small girl playing hopscotch by herself on the walk in front of a deserted house. I was always like that. Alone. Everybody out here on the razor edge of survival trying to claim respectability but us—Old Annie, Ruthie Nevada, Mamie, Cherise. We had to stick together. Ruthie being a working woman, Annie being crazy, Cher and Mamie just being themselves, loving each other since they lived in Mississippi. Then Mamie's strange politics, the way she could drink gin and let no God in our house—slap after slap in the faces of the proper colored on Rondo Street. Mamie was a Garveyite, a Communist, a thug, a pinko, a bull dagger, a nigger red. What could be worse? To have all those things let you down, I guess. To watch everything fail you but your lover. Cherise never failed her. But by the time Mamie was dying something had broken her heart right out.

I don't know much about love but I do know it can kill because it killed Cherise. She and Mamie were all I had and when they were gone, I was alone again. Except for Emma. Emma Nevada coming to my rescue. But she was always thinking about me, making her plans. When we were kids, we'd race to my house to listen to radio programs, and every night, Emma'd run backwards all the way to the corner shouting, goodnight, Liberty Grace, see you in the morning. Making her plans. What would have happened to me without my Emma? Keeping me in mind, keeping me around, keeping me out of trouble. We're so close, I can hear her talking to me though we don't say a word. I wonder what she and Henry fought about this time.

The sun beat through the windshield and onto Liberty's skin. Hot. Humidity turned the horizon white. Liberty turned in her seat. "Let's go to Dairy Queen."

Emma smiled at her.

"Terry Cee, we're going to the bank first to cash my paycheck, then get us some ice cream. My treat."

"Right on, sister," he grinned, taking a sharp left.

"What did you get?" Fat Huey asked Isra as they squatted down on the sidewalk back home.

"I got a Buster Bar. So did Emma. Ricki wanted a Suicide Slush, but Liberty said it sounded disgusting so she got a dip cone instead."

Rickshaw said nothing. She was busy burning up ants with a magnifying glass.

Isra, Ricki and Fat Huey were stuck playing on Banfield Street. They got chased out of the cemetery that morning, and the caretaker said if he caught them in there again, they'd be staying. They were only trying to see if Fat Huey could make a dead body pop out of the ground like a banana did its peel by jumping on a new grave. They stopped by the playground, but the big boys who smoked and rode stingray bicycles were there. The three of them wandered down to the empty lot, where the Dropiks and some other kids were tying a rope swing to a huge oak tree.

"And if I catch any of you kids playing on this rope, I'll hang you with it," Jackie Dropik said, leaning into Isra's face.

Ricki got lucky with a punch that sent Jackie Dropik to his knees, eyes bulging and not a sound coming from his mouth.

"Did you kill him?" Isra asked, panting from their running escape.

"I don't know," Ricki replied, gulping down air. "But if he ever tries to touch you, you let me know."

"Your hand is bleeding."

"Scraped it on his zipper." Rickshaw clenched her fist, spit on her knuckles, then rubbed them on her shorts.

Ricki shut the torn-up guitar case. Maybe Liberty'd get me a new one for our birthdays, she speculated, turning out the light and walking out of her room. Maybe she'll lend me the money for one. "I'll be at Boff's," she said to Israellen who still hadn't moved from the couch but to go to the bathroom.

"Think Liberty will get a TV if I asked her?"

"She might since she's feeling so sorry for you."

Isra kept on looking at the ceiling.

"Need anything while I'm out?"

Isra shook her head. Just get out of my sight, she thought. The back door slammed shut. Fuck you, Rickshaw. I hate you sometimes. Everything goes your way, you never get hurt, you never do the wrong thing. Isra sat up on the couch, the muscles in her arms vibrating like one of Ricki's guitar strings. Slowly, she struggled to her feet. Damn it. Her knee throbbed in spite of the painkillers. Grabbing a crutch, she hobbled out to the kitchen. Easy, she thought, gripping the back of a chair with both hands, the crutch clattering to the floor. She lifted her leg from her hip, her calf and foot feeling like dead weight while a fine layer of sweat broke out on her face. Damn. She struggled to regain her balance. No more painkillers, she thought. Auditions are two months away, and I have to stay limber. Isra straightened her back and lifted again.

Late that night when Ricki came out of her room, she found Isra balancing on one foot, hand gripping that same chair. "If you don't get that arm right, Madame will throw you out a window and break your other leg."

Isra, saying nothing, stretched her arm up.

Ricki took the milk from the refrigerator. "Want some?"

"No."

"Good for bones."

Isra stretched.

Ricki shrugged. "Sure you should be doing that?"

"I have to."

Wish I'd brought a guitar or a boom box, Ricki thought, squinting at a gull circling above the sand dunes, a speck against the huge sky. She shifted the duffle bag to her other shoulder. I feel great, I feel wonderful, could almost break into one of those old dance moves, time step, double pull-back, double wings. I never could dance, barely managed to riff or shuffle, but I feel like I could do all those steps now, just soft-shoe my way through the sand. She breathed deeply. Can almost taste the ocean in the air.

What happened to us, me and my baby sister? Seems I turned around and she was gone, just like that song by Dion. Abraham, Martin and Israellen Jones going over the hill like their pants were on fire. Not that she's dead, hell, I wonder if that makes a difference at all. Seems like the dead are here as much as anything else, it's just that all us living people ignore them. Strange thing, dying is. Sometimes it's expected, it ought to happen, like when somebody gets buried in a building after an earthquake. Fourteen, fifteen days and out that person walks. And other times it's like Charlie King getting kicked in the head where his steel plate was and dying on the sidewalk right then. I don't think it's the dying that bugs people. It's the leaving. Maybe that's why announcers tell how many people have died over a holiday weekend, to let others know they got away this time. They don't have to pack up someone's clothes and watch the trash collectors haul it away in big garbage bags.

When Liberty died, I thought I could handle my part of the arrangements. Gave Liberty's stuff away, sold the house and Isra went back to London. I took the cats—the cobalt blue and Tina Turner—and did all right till Tina Turner died two months later. I came home and there she was. I've never seen anything so still in my life. And that night I felt my heart shatter like Liberty's glass cat. I realized I got a life as fragile as glass. And this one thing keeps me wondering—how long before something else shatters it? And is that why Isra and I keep reaching for music and dancing and acting? There's a certainty in being a star, any kind of star.

Isra an actor. I never believed it until I saw her working with words as hard as she worked those ballet steps. Must've been the draw of the stage that started her, maybe she thought she should keep performing till her leg got better. But her dancing time was over. Forever. I swear I could almost hear Liberty's heart break when Isra got hurt. But who really knows about Liberty? Seemed her heart, like that little glass cat, had been broken and reglued so many times, it got easier to leave the pieces in a box and wait for Emma Nevada's return.

Three

At the top of the dune, a cry of laughter carried on the wind as it rushed through Isra's hair. She smiled, her mouth clean of the taste of blood and the color red. There was a ruin hidden in the mountains. It must have been huge once. A fortress against everything but God. Now it's empty and everything rushes to destroy it, but the arches still give a feeling of grace and protection. You could count on something like an arch. There's something all-encompassing about it, as if patterned after the dome of heaven. If there is a heaven. If there is a God. Liberty used to think God was a cat. A kitten constantly fooling around with a ball of string known as the universe, knotting up things that would otherwise have no notion of each other.

I don't think there is a God. For all the churches and books and stories, it's the fear of death that makes people wish for a hereafter. Some people say that just thinking of someone brings her back to life, back to eat and breathe and make love all over again. Eternal life is repetition. Me, I think life is all inexact replica. Look at Liberty and Ricki and me. Look what we all inherited—strength of mind, independence, art, talent. But it's not exactly the same. Things changed in the mix from Mamie and Cherise to Liberty and Emma to me and Rickshaw.

I wonder if all daughters return to their mothers. I keep turning to Liberty and to Emma with thousands of questions and doubts. Liberty and Emma had a better handle on love than most and now I wish one or the other would somehow explain to me how it works. Maybe Caleb and I—Caleb and I will never work this out. We disagree about fidelity. I want him to be true to me in his heart, in his mind, in his time. What does it mean to fall in love? I think Emma and Liberty knew. They knew how to be true.

"Now listen," Emma said, looking from one twin to the other sitting on the floor at her feet. "*I woke up this morning with an awful aching head—*" she sang. "*Woke up this morning with an awful aching head—*"

"Your voice is funny," Ricki interrupted.

"Well, see if you can sing it better, smart mouth," Emma shot back.

"Who's it by? Diana Ross?" Isra asked.

"Bessie Smith. Bessie Smith sang it."

Five years since the twins had seen her and they were shy at first, knowing they should remember but couldn't. But Emma oohed over Isra's dancing and showed Ricki some tricks on her beat-up acoustic guitar. As the days went on, Emma let Isra and Ricki wear her dashikis as dresses and her long hoop earrings which Isra wore over her own ears and once Ricki stuck one in her nose. Emma wore glasses now that magnified her eyes from beautiful to startling. "Far-sighted. I'm getting old."

"So's the rest of the world," Liberty replied, stacking up the clean dishes and putting them into the cupboard.

Emma pushed away the newspaper she'd been reading. "Things are getting bad, Liberty Grace. Things are turning out the way I feared. Nobody's listening to us anymore."

"I told you a hundred years ago nobody was going to listen—interferes with their own talking."

"We've done some good, Liberty, we have. Just now everybody's stopped thinking and started throwing stones," she mumbled, getting up from the table wearily.

Liberty quietly followed her out of the kitchen, watching

Emma as she disappeared into Isra's room. Was a time nothing bothered her. Now silver threads flickered in her halo of hair and the lines around her eyes and mouth weren't from laughing. "Girls?"

Isra looked up from the book. She was sitting in Liberty's chair calmly reading to Ricki, who was lying on her belly on the floor. Both of them were wearing their yellow pajamas and looked so innocent, like little chicks, she thought, fuzzy newborns right out of the egg.

"What's that you're reading?"

"Library book," Ricki answered.

Liberty reached for the book. *Miss Bessie: The Story of Bessie Smith.* "Is it any good?"

Isra pursed her lips. "Yeah," she said, nodding after a moment.

"Well, you keep reading, honey." Liberty handed back the book, lay down on the couch and closed her eyes.

Later, when the twins were asleep and Liberty sat in the kitchen alone, Emma came back out with a bottle and a dart gun. She set the bottle on the table with a clunk and grabbed two glasses from the cupboard. "Got any tape?"

"Top drawer to the left of the stove."

She took out the roll and unfolded a creased magazine picture. "I've been wanting to do this since *Life* magazine put him into living color," Emma said, taping the page to the wall. She loaded the small gun, spitting on the suction cup to make the dart stick better, took aim and shot LBJ right in his face. It stuck. "Bull's eye."

"While you're playing shoot-out at the OK Corral, mind if I pour us a drink?"

"That's what it's for," Emma said, loading another dart. "And if we finish this bottle, I got another. Got enough booze to send Noah looking for his ark."

Liberty poured whiskey into the two glasses.

With a snick, the second dart hit and bounced off. She loaded the third and spat on the end. "You know, I hate that man, just for being what he is. Rich. White. Southern."

"He's doing us good, Emma."

"I expect good from him like I expect Stepin Fetchit to pull into town on the Underground Railroad." She pulled the trigger and hit him in the hairline. "If you want to try, you'll have to get the darts."

Liberty sipped some whiskey, letting it burn like a line of fire all the way down her throat. "No, thanks. I don't like guns."

"I don't like guns either, but maybe Huey P. Newton is right, maybe it is the only way."

"Live by a gun and you'll die by it, Emma."

She set the dart gun quietly on the table and picked up her glass. "I never thought you'd be signifying biblical, Liberty Grace."

"It's not biblical. It's a fact."

Emma gazed into her glass then turned to Liberty. "I know. I know that. If I was a man maybe I could forget it, and buy me a rifle and all the bullets in the world. Hell, even being a woman is barely enough to make me hesitate."

"So why do you?"

"I keep remembering Mama working down on the corner. Ruthie the whore fucking the soldiers from Fort Snelling in her bedroom with the pink light bulb. There's something about men carrying guns, thinking they're bad because they carry two weapons—one strapped to their back and the other hanging between their legs. These young brothers think the way to run the world is by using guns and that makes me hesitate." Emma stretched so far her back cracked. "I am worn out."

"What are you doing in that room, anyway?"

"Restitching memories. Writing. Waiting for inspiration. I wait all the time, for the bus, for the cops, wait for everything. Every time I go South, I'm waiting again. I wait for some redneck to find the biggest, blackest, blue-gum in the county, strip him, whip him and make him whistle 'Dixie' while crawling around the Confederate flag."

"Don't think so hard on that idea, or else somebody will read your mind and try it."

Emma giggled. "Remember when we used to practice reading each other's minds with a deck of cards? Remember that one time you got twenty-seven in a row? I thought you were magic or something. Voodoo gal, my mama always called you. You were a voodoo gal. I don't know where she thought that up."

"People from Louisiana always have strange ideas."

"I suppose. Mama did have some strange things in her head. All my life she'd tell me, you got to stand up and be counted. Be counted, be somebody. Henry went in the Army, came back to sell cars and now everybody thinks he's bourgeois and respectable, won't even talk to me or Dee. Poor Delia. We're the most disrespected people I know. We are getting counted, me and her, but only on the casualty list. She's strung out on Selby Avenue, and all I got is nightmares, cheap whiskey and the courage to stand up, only to find out most of the time I'm standing alone. Do you know what that makes my ass? A target. For both sides."

A new bitterness was buried in her like a bullet in the woodwork; it had worked its way just far enough for Liberty to get a peak at its shiny edge.

"Always waiting. All my life I've had to talk to a white man with one foot in the air ready to run. Now this one," she nodded her head at LBJ, "thinks he's got a peaceful solution. Well, LBJ and Doctor Martin Luther King Junior got another think coming. They can depend on a little bit of difficulty."

Liberty looked over her glass. "You're not getting into anything you shouldn't, are you?"

"Of course not, Liberty Grace. I never get into anything I shouldn't." Emma reached for the bottle and splashed more whiskey into her glass. "Want some more?"

Liberty shook her head, swallowed the rest in her glass and grimaced. Feels like a forest fire's started in my stomach.

"Do you know what the little brothers call Dr. King? They

call him de Lawd. They stand at the back of the crowd and scream: here come de Lawd, here come de Lawd." Emma slammed back her whiskey and picked up the bottle again.

"Put it down, Emma. It's too late for this and even if you were making sense, I couldn't understand you. Time for bed." Liberty stood up, her ankle and knee aching, and lay her hand on Emma's shoulder. She better not be in a resisting frame of mind; between my kids and her revolutions, I've just about had it.

"It's time we quit being so nice. No more waiting. Time we quit being little lost sheep for someone to gather up so he can win a bright shiny Nobel Peace Prize."

"He's trying, Emma. I heard him on the radio. Now would you get up?" Liberty lifted her arm.

"You heard him on the radio, heard his dreaming and his preaching. You heard him. You and your radio, always got to have it on like it was your skin, like if all that noise wasn't going your insides would fall out all over the kitchen floor. Would you stop pulling on me? A woman's got a right to stand on her own two feet."

"Then, woman, get up and get your ass to bed."

Emma slowly stood up, taking the bottle with her. "You got a filthy mouth, you know that?"

"Em?" Liberty stopped outside Isra's room. "Would you rather sleep with me tonight?"

"Yes. But you got to borrow me a nightgown. There are children around and we can't be having them finding me naked in the sack with you."

"Sure, baby."

Emma pushed open the bedroom door. "You know that little match girl story? She's freezing to death and lights up all her matches? That's what we remind me of, all of us Afro-Americans." She leaned heavy on the last word. "I'm telling you Liberty Grace, it's time all the little lost match girls got themselves organized and burned the whole rotten thing to the ground. I want it finished."

"All your talk." Liberty turned on the small lamp on the nightstand. And all my ghosts start standing before me when you say these things, so many their arms and legs start overlapping.

"Mamie didn't think there was going to be any other way," Emma said softly.

Liberty pulled a neatly folded nightgown out of her drawer. "What did you or anybody else know what Mamie Fortune was thinking?"

"Some things I know. Remember when those boys followed us home from school screaming obscenities at us?"

"I remember how you tried to fight all of them at once."

"If you'd been a little bigger, we would've whipped their butts. Weren't doing too bad as it was."

Liberty sat down and untied her shoes. "Then Mamie came tearing down the street, picked those boys up and planted one size eleven boot in their behinds, one right after another. Didn't even set down her lunch box."

Emma plopped on the other side of the bed, the whiskey sloshing in the bottle. "And after dinner, she walked down Rondo Street to my house and taught me how to box the right way."

"Scientific fighting, she called it. If it doesn't work, kick them in the balls."

"Only fight if there's no way out, she'd say. Your best line of defense is fast legs and a good pair of shoes. I remember her getting arrested, you remember?"

"I ended up down at your house and your mama left us to earn bail. Nineteen forty-three, it was. I remember because Mamie had me memorize the 'Draftee's Prayer' for school recitation. Mrs. Thomas got so mad, she banned me from Patriotism Day."

"And Delia got one of her boyfriends to do something to the lights so they wouldn't stop blinking on and off."

"They never did find out who did it, did they?"

"Cherise did."

"Cherise found out everything."

Emma sighed and kicked off her shoes. "Liberty?"

"Hmm?" she answered, rubbing her ankle.

"You ever think of doing it with a woman?"

"Doing what?" Liberty stood up and began taking off her clothes.

"You know." Emma set the bottle on the nightstand.

"What got you wondering about that?" she asked, standing in her slip.

"Thinking of Mamie and Cherise. Them being funny. Well?" she demanded, staring at Liberty. "Have you? Ever wanted to make love with another woman, I mean."

"Why are you asking me this?"

"What if I was to tell you I did?"

"Then I would tell you, Emma Nevada," Liberty picked up the dress off the floor, walked to the closet and took out a hanger, "that I love you like no other, but there are some things you better learn to hide about yourself before you get shot." She hung up her dress and shut the closet door.

Emma cracked a grin. "Maybe you're right, Liberty Grace."

Liberty peeled off her slip. "Let's go to sleep. Please?"

"Ain't you afraid to take your clothes off in front of me?"

"Why should I be?" She unhooked her bra and let it slide down her arms. "You know I keep a gun."

Emma leaned back against the headboard and swung her legs up on the bed. "I don't want to go to sleep. I want to talk. I feel like we're running out of time."

"You're not off to do something dangerous, are you?"

"Right now is a dangerous place to live, Liberty. Everything I do is a little revolution, just being alive is a miracle of rebellion."

"I know that, Emma." Liberty let the cotton nightgown fall around her body.

"Yes," she said softly, "I believe you do. More than anybody."

Liberty walked around to the far side of the bed. "Okay,

what do you want to talk about?"

"Nothing in particular. Let's just talk." Emma reached for the whiskey bottle and took a swallow. "I never drink when I'm in the field. Too dangerous. Them college kids don't understand that. They think danger always comes head-on, that you can get out of the way. They don't know a thing about the South."

Liberty fluffed her pillow and got in bed. The clean sheets felt good. "Is that where you're always going?"

"Sometimes." Emma unhooked her overalls and pushed them off, then unbuttoned her shirt. "I'm sort of a refugee in my own country, wandering in every direction."

"Put on your nightgown, Emma."

"People down South, I don't understand them. They're not like us," she continued, standing up to wobble around barebreasted in the small bedroom. "They stay in that hate-infested place."

Liberty shrugged.

"Aw, forget it," Emma mumbled, snatching up the nightgown and pulling it over her head. "Little short. A little tight."

"You want another?"

"Naw. I'm a little tight myself. Get it?" She struggled with the gown for a moment. "I'm serious. I don't understand why they stay."

"Maybe they don't want to be refugees like you and lose the little they have."

"Lose everything but their accents," Emma said, getting into bed.

"And the chance to go home."

"Who'd want to call it home? I think they're just too afraid to tell themselves the truth."

"You always said truth was in the eye of the beholder."

"What's in my eye is the biggest, whitest, send-you-to-hell lie I ever seen."

"Then stop looking."

Emma rubbed her face. Hers was a very ordinary black arm

with a beautiful pink palm attached. "I don't think I can stop looking. It's what holds us together."

"The fight?"

"The defeat. Our own defeat."

Liberty sighed and turned off the small lamp. "Whiskey is bad business, Emma. Sleep it off and we'll come back to this in the morning."

"It is morning. And it's all bad business. If it weren't for the whiskey—I got a theory that most of us got here because of a bottle of booze on the weekend. Most of us are Saturday Night Specials," she giggled and her voice faded. "Where's my guitar? Let's make some music. Let's pretend it's the Fifties again. Let's sing 'The Clock' by Johnny Ace. Remember him? What a voice. You ready?"

"No."

Emma flopped further under the single sheet that covered them. "Remember when Marcus Garvey died? When was that?"

"Nineteen forty. June tenth." Liberty opened her eyes.

"Nineteen forty? You sure? That long ago. Wow. You wore black that day, remember? All black, skirt, stockings—I don't know where you got that blouse but it practically hung to your knees."

"I told you it was Mamie's."

"We switched shirts so I could wear black, too." Emma shook her head in the darkness. "Maybe Marcus Garvey had the right idea, maybe we should all go back to Africa."

"You, maybe," Liberty shut her eyes, hoping to keep them that way. "I think Africans would consider me a tourist with a good tan."

"You been getting darker."

"My age. Some morning I'm going to wake up a complete stranger to myself." The room went quiet. Maybe she'll fall asleep, Liberty hoped.

Emma started humming. "What is that song?"

"What song?"

"This one." She hummed again. "I can't remember it. Mamie'd play it on the Victrola all the time."

"That was a regular record player, not a Victrola. We're not that old. And it's 'I'd Rather Be Dead and Buried in My Grave.' You'll be hearing it when Ricki decides to play disc jockey first thing in the morning. Go to sleep."

"You heard Aretha Franklin?"

Liberty opened her eyes and lifted her head to stare at Emma. "I'm not the one stuck in the sticks, sister. Of course I've heard Aretha."

"Great, isn't she?" Emma started singing, "*Ooh, whatchoo want—*"

"Emma?" Liberty interrupted.

"Yeah?"

"I think you should just stick to guitar playing."

"That's what your kid thinks, too."

It was an accident. Really. No one thought the cat would break like it did, in fact, neither Ricki nor Isra thought there was even a chance that the Nerf football Emma gave them could hurt it or anything else. When the Nerf bounced off Ricki's forehead because she couldn't catch it, hopped over the dried flower arrangement and knocked over the cobalt-blue cat, even then they thought they'd just pick it up and put it back and get on with playing the Vikings versus the Packers in the living room.

"What are we going to do?" Isra asked, holding the bottom half of the glass cat.

"I don't know," her twin answered, picking up the top.

"Can we fix it?"

Ricki shrugged. "Come on."

Isra knocked twice on the bedroom door before the typewriter stopped inside.

"This better be important," Emma bellowed. "Well?"

Ricki glanced at Isra, who was looking at her. Slowly, each extended her fist and opened her hand.

"We're sorry," Isra said.

Emma picked up the two pieces. "You're in trouble now."

"We didn't mean to," Ricki said.

She studied the broken cat. "You know, it's not busted too bad. It's just broke in half."

The twins looked up at her.

"There's some glue under the sink," Isra said hopefully.

"I'll get it." Ricki dashed off.

The cat sat on the kitchen table to dry.

"Say your prayers to the great god Elmer and don't either one of you touch it. Next time, play football in the basement— nothing down there worth fixing if it gets broke." Emma smiled to ease the irritation out of her voice.

"Think it'll be okay?" Isra asked.

"Yeah," Ricki answered confidently.

"Think Liberty will know?"

"What's that cat doing here?" Liberty asked as soon as she walked into the kitchen.

"Emma put it there," Ricki said.

"Why?"

"To dry."

"What?"

"To dry. The glue had to dry."

"What glue?"

"The glue to fix it."

"Why did it need fixing?"

"It got broke."

"How did it get broke?"

"It fell."

"It fell. Did one of you knock it over?"

"No. It got hit by something."

Liberty folded her arms and nodded her head. "And what, Rickshaw Jones, did it get hit with?"

"With the Nerf."

"Uh huh. Did the Nerf just fly through the air all on its own and knock this over?"

"No."

"Then how?"

"I didn't catch it."

"You two were playing in the living room again, weren't you?"

"Yes."

"Okay." Liberty lifted out a chicken defrosting in the sink. "Ricki, no records for you today or tomorrow. Isra, extra tap classes and no ballet. If either one of you pouts, the punishment is doubled."

"But Liberty—"

"It was a accident—"

"Shush. Just shush," she said, turning on the radio.

Lady sings the blues...

The bathtub gurgled. What an ugly sound, Israellen thought, setting a lid on the pan. The back door flew open, followed by a blast of arctic air.

"Damn, it's cold," Ricki shouted. "You been outside, baby sister?"

"How stupid do you think I am?"

"You really want me to answer that?" Ricki grinned and slammed the door shut with her behind. She leaned a battered guitar case against the wall and unsnapped her jacket. The buzz from the dope gave her a little wiggle in her walk over to the refrigerator. "Should've heard us today, we were jamming. Papa May had us smash gospel and reggae together. You should've seen those white boys trying to bob their knees in time to the music. Liberty home?"

Isra nodded and took the pan off the stove. "Why don't you take your shoes off before you spatter snow everywhere?"

"Jesus, who died and made you Aunt Jemima?"

"Just do it."

Ricki kicked her tennis shoes off and they landed right next to Liberty's boots. "Damn." Ricki gritted her teeth. "I hate

93

stepping on snow in my stocking feet—gives my foot an ice cream headache."

"Hungry?"

"What you making? Mmm, hot dogs. You could get a bit more adventurous in your cooking, Israellen." Grabbing her guitar, she skipped out of the kitchen. Ooh, Billie Holiday on the stereo. Good choice, Liberty Grace. Ricki pulled out one of her albums, and soon Bessie Smith's voice filled the room.

Tell me what's wrong with me...

Flipping the light switch in her room, Ricki yanked off her jacket. She set the guitar case on the bed and took the guitar out carefully. You beautiful thing, you, she thought, leaning it in its usual place next to the dresser. She took a plastic bag of dope out of the pick carrier. You're beautiful, too, she thought, dropping it in the top drawer of her dresser.

"You ever coming out of there, Liberty?" she shouted at the bathroom door as she walked back down the hall.

I'm sad as I can be...

Isra limped out of the kitchen and peered around the wall. "Do you have to play that old record?"

"Yep."

"Can't you play anything different?"

"Nope."

Still I made up my mind...

Isra crossed her arms and walked back into the kitchen. If I have to listen to the blues all night again I will scream. She speared a hot dog with a fork and tossed it on a piece of bread she had on a plate. Damn Ricki, she'll play this record over and over all night long, just like she did when we were little. Her stomach started to twist, as if someone was playing hula-hoop with her intestines.

To find someone who will treat me kind...

"How's the leg?"

Isra dropped the fork. It bounced on the tiled floor to Ricki's feet. "If you don't stop sneaking up on me, you're going to be asking about my heart pretty soon."

"Sorry." Rickshaw picked up the fork and tossed it in the sink, wiping away the grease with her toe.

No matter how cruel he may be, it won't be you...

"Well?"

"Well what?" Isra grabbed another fork out of the drawer.

"How's the leg?" Ricki repeated, pulling open the refrigerator. No beer.

Israellen twitched her shoulders.

"What the hell does this mean?" asked Ricki, imitating her.

Isra said nothing.

He may beat me and break my heart, but it won't be you...

"What's the matter, prima donna, you break your tongue trying to eat the food you cooked?"

Isra slammed her plate on the counter.

"Hey, I was just asking." What is wrong with this silly bitch? she wondered, walking out of the kitchen.

He may love me and treat me kind...

Ricki took the needle off the record, turned on the radio and walked back to her own room. Jesus, Isra's freaking out— must be going nuts with nothing to do but go to school. She flopped onto her bed and turned on the radio and the small lamp on the nightstand. The phone rang in the other room and she paused, listening. Guess it ain't for me, she decided, resting her head in her hands. Nobody ever calls me unless I got to get somebody out of trouble.

Liberty watched the small whirlpool as the last of the water emptied from the tub. Looks like the twister in *The Wizard of Oz*, she thought absently. She dried off her arms and glanced in the mirror. One single blue vein arched through her left breast. Its path was clear through her skin, as blue and curved as a secondary road on a Rand-McNally road map, like the one I got when I drove to Mississippi to see Bub's farm. What a strange place, that farm was so dry and filled with weeds like the land wasn't giving anything to anybody out of sheer stubbornness.

The vein disappeared near her nipple. Like the road just

ends here, she thought, tracing the branching line. I remember when that vein first started to show so clear. When I breast-fed my girls. Kept that up though the nurse at the hospital said everyone was bottle feeding their babies now. I knew my milk was better for them, why else would I have it and I sure had plenty for both of them till they were almost two years old. I was strong then, could juggle both of them at the same time and think nothing of it. Like Cherise always said, you learn to cope when you have to.

Liberty wiped off the water on her belly and dried her legs, the right one looking a little thinner than the left, the old scar a patch of white against her skin. Like the crystallized sugar in the honey jar, she thought. But still muscled, which is good. Looking okay for an old lady, she thought, staring critically in the mirror. Flipping the towel to her back with both hands, she scrubbed down her back, the rough edge scratching the last itches on her skin, then wrapped the bathrobe around her and cleaned out the tub. "Ricki, why don't you come out of that room and join us at the dinner table?" she called, rubbing lotion into her hands and elbows.

Ricki leaned her guitar back against the wall. Goddamn, can't get any practice in this house, how they expect me to be a star?

"Sit down here and eat," Liberty said as she walked into the kitchen.

"I ain't hungry," she replied, opening the cupboard.

"Then have a glass of milk and be civilized."

"We got any dessert?"

"Some ice cream in the freezer, though god knows how you can eat ice cream when it's this cold. Isra, quit picking and eat your food."

Isra set her fork down. "I'm going to go do my homework."

As she limped out of the kitchen, Ricki sat down in her place. "What's wrong with her?"

"Nothing. Should there be?"

Ricki shrugged, picked up Isra's lukewarm hot dog and took a bite.

"Use a fork, please."

Ricki jumped up to get the ketchup. "She wants a TV."

"She's not getting one," Liberty replied between chews. "Get that cat off the table, please."

Rickshaw scooped up Tina Turner and dropped her on the floor. "Want some hot dog?" she asked the cat, tearing off a small piece.

"If that cat doesn't eat that, you clean it up. How's the band?"

"Okay. I don't think I'm supposed to play reggae."

"You got the hair for it."

Ricki stuffed the last part of the hot dog in her mouth and just managed to mumble, "They do too many drugs."

"You better not be doing any drugs."

"I'm not."

"You better not."

"I got plans, Liberty, I don't need that kind of shit messing me up."

"You better keep that in mind, girl."

"I do. Geez," Ricki said, setting the plate in the sink and walking out.

Isra was lying on the couch in her usual place, reading a script.

"Good hot dog," Ricki said, plopping into Liberty's recliner. Tina Turner jumped into her lap.

"Glad you liked it." Isra turned a page.

Ricki glanced at the top of her sister's head. Isra's got beautiful hair, all shiny like someone painted it on. "What are you doing?"

"Memorizing my lines. I'm Juliet in *Romeo and Juliet*."

"That Juliet's a white girl. Why are you always playing white girls?"

"I don't pick the plays, Ricki."

"So what? What's the matter, the teacher too lazy to go out looking for plays with black people?"

"Durben thinks it's important to study the classics. Shakespeare is as classic as you can get." Isra tossed the script onto the floor and looked through the curtain sheers. Outside, the snow lay flat with night pouring itself drop by drop onto Banfield Street. "Besides, Shakespeare wrote plays with black people in them—*Othello*, for instance."

"Huh. He was probably a murderer or something." Ricki looked skeptical. "If you're done with memorizing, you could do my homework."

"Not on your life."

"For a smart chick like you, it'll take two seconds."

"No."

"Oh, come on. Don't be such a drag. I'll give you five bucks."

"No, Rickshaw."

Ricki shrugged. She didn't even look at me. Hell, just trying to get her interested in stuff. "Hey, want to hear the reggae song the band wrote today?"

"I do," Liberty said, walking into the living room, her cup of tea still steaming.

"Great. I'll go get the tape." Ricki brushed the cat off her lap and dashed out of the room.

Liberty set her cup on the end table. "Are you sure you're not hungry, Israellen?" she asked, drawing the curtain closed.

Isra crossed her arms. Just leave me alone, she thought as Ricki bounced back into the room.

"We kind of ripped off an old gospel tune," she said, shoving the cassette into the tape deck. "But it sounds pretty good, if you like reggae."

Liberty sat down in her chair. "When's your first gig?"

"With Papa May? I don't know. Man, he's always saying it's going to be next month but nothing ever happens." Wonder if we'll ever get any gigs, she thought, listening to the background chatter on the tape. Probably not. Papa May counted down and the intro began. *Ezekiel saw the wheel...*

Too ragged, she decided, and the other guitar is still off. White boys don't get it. Reggae beat isn't counted off, it's just an agreement between the band to build the music on. She shook her head. I wouldn't let my band play in public if I was Papa May, either.

Way in the middle of the air...

My band will be perfect, dead on for every note. Not like this or the punk band, either. Shit, those boys sound like radio static during a thunderstorm—no matter if every instrument is out of tune and nobody but me has rhythm. Why do I even stick it out with them? Got to learn to play everything and everybody.

"You got to learn how to play a man going up the stairs and don't break into a scale." Yaz lit a Lucky Strike, letting a cloud of blue smoke into the room. "Don't you even try that cliché with me, though you're going to be playing clichés for a long time before you get to play yourself. You empty yourself of all that hero worship. Got to get over wanting to play like Wes Montgomery, T-Bone Walker, Django Reinhart or Jimi Hendrix."

"Or B. B. King?"

"Him you hang onto. And Leadbelly. If you start playing like them, then we'll know we're getting somewhere."

Play fast, play slow, get myself a job doing everybody else every night and then one day, Yaz says, I blow it apart. Tear it all open. And the blues comes from what's left standing. So I play every kind of music to find my own. And for stage experience. Get up in front of people and learn how to handle anything from crummy sound to crummy musicians, like my punkers. Those white boys don't got any pride, they don't care if they're any good, they want to scream and jump around and stick their tongues out at people.

Ricki walked from the bus stop to Boff's. His parents were at Lake Tahoe and the house was his till they came back, meaning it was time for their first gig. She flipped up her collar; the night was cool and a little humid, typical for May, and passed the guitar case from her left to right hand. The setting sun turned the sky orange to purple to deep blue above the proud houses. Used to be a rich neighborhood, Ricki thought, glancing at them above the steep green yards that gave each the feel of money. From one, a small white face appeared behind a second-story window. Go to sleep now, kid, Ricki thought, shuffling up the walk to Boff's. You won't be sleeping after we start playing.

She walked into cigarette smoke and a living room hot from everyone being smashed against one another with the stereo blasting the Buzzcocks' "Orgasm Addict." Lots of people and they're all white, she realized, leaning against her guitar case. Goddamn, I am surrounded again. Geez, and it stinks. Why do punkers always smell so bad? Looking around, Ricki locked eyes with a white woman sitting on the end of the couch. Her face was narrow and in the glare of the multi-colored lights Boff had set up in the living room, she couldn't tell the color of her hair. Ricki's fingers twitched along with the song wailing out of the stereo. Hell, maybe her hair's green, she thought, her shoulder blades beginning to tighten as if getting ready to be hit. Her heart squeezed a beat. I think somebody's throwing a pass my way. Not in so many words. But I can catch it. A crowd of six or seven people staggered between them, blocking Ricki's view. By the time they moved, the small woman was gone. Damn, didn't even have a chance to introduce myself.

Someone gripped her arm. Her heart squeezed a beat again. Maybe her? Maybe, she thought, turning slowly. It was Clyde.

She nodded at him. Over by the wall near the stereo stood the small woman, sipping from her glass and smiling slightly as she stared.

"We're setting up in back," he shouted over the music.

Ricki nodded again. She's a good-looking babe, she decided, for a honky. Hair shoulder-length, her eyes pale and a pair of Ray Bans hanging from her collar. She was thin, a little too thin, but cute. Then, as Rickshaw Jones stared at them, the woman's nipples budded under the tight Led Zeppelin t-shirt she was wearing. Damn, Ricki's breath seemed knocked out of her. What a good trick *that* is.

Clyde squeezed her arm again. "Come on."

He led her out the front door and around to the backyard.

"Hey, baby, what's happening?" Boff asked, his hair corkscrewing in every direction. He was setting up his drums on the wooden deck off the house. "Keg in the downstairs bathroom and there's bottles in the cooler."

Setting her guitar down, Ricki got a bottle and threw the cap into the grass. Boff had his drums up, but the rest of the gear was laying all over the place, the cables snaking out in every direction. The PA was sitting on a card table that sank under its weight. A stack of chrome over by the steps was the microphone stands. Clyde's keyboard was leaning against a speaker cabinet. What a mess. She shook her head.

"It's Barry's fault," Clyde said, now pushing the other speaker cabinet into place. "He took off with the truck this afternoon so we had to move the stuff in my car."

"Why didn't you come get me?"

"Your sister said you were jamming with Papa May."

She'd been trying to jam on a different kind of music with Jinna Johnson, who wouldn't go any further than necking, for god's sake. Who ever heard of an eighteen-year-old dyke not having the guts to take off her clothes? "Where's Barry now?"

"Upstairs getting high."

Christ. She grabbed an end of the speaker cabinet and helped Clyde slide it across the deck. An hour and a half later, she was tuned up and ready for a sound check. Ricki moved her guitar board one last time. Reverb, Chorus, Overdrive, Vibrato, that was the order of the effects boxes; she memorized them the first time she and Barry cut out the hunk of plywood to fit them all in. She spent three months figuring them all out and now could hear them all in any variation, in any order. Cranking the volume of her guitar, she wailed off a short solo.

Sounds terrible. She stepped on the Overdrive button and tried again.

"Sounds great, baby," Boffo called.

"Barry, your bass is still out of tune."

He belched. "Only fascists tune."

"Give it here, I'll do it." She swung her guitar strap over her head and took the bass. E, A, D, G, there it is, she thought, cocking her head as she walked a blues progression up and down the neck. Very fine. She handed the instrument back to Barry, who smiled a little crookedly. "You ready boys?"

Clyde grinned from behind his electric piano, his teeth long and white like the keys.

They'd never played in front of anyone before, she realized. Out in the yard small clusters of people stood around in various stages of drunkenness, their hands in their pockets. Holy shit, Ricki thought, they are waiting to hear us. Her throat suddenly felt like it was going to close in on her and she was glad Barry had to sing the first song, the Stranglers' "Something Better Change." At least it's short, and with only three chords, we can't screw it up too bad.

At the break she slammed a beer even before she set down her guitar. We suck. Something really wrong about playing for people when you're not ready for it. Tossing the empty bottle into a box, she set her guitar carefully in its case then plopped down in a lawn chair with another beer and a cigarette. We are so terrible, I can't believe it. As if anyone even noticed or cared. She stared through the smoke at nothing. No wonder these jerks want to turn the volume up after every song; if it's loud enough, no one will realize how crummy we are. Someday, I swear to god, she thought, with *someday* looming up at her like the lid of a coffin, someday, I'll have a drummer with rhythm, a bass player with pitch and a sound system that can carry my voice. And no more white-boy-from-the-suburbs-thinking-he's-a-rebel garbage. I'll play my music, whatever that turns out to be. For now, I'll just keep listening and listening, going every which way, leaving musical ideas behind like dead bodies, though right now, I'd be happiest leaving these guys behind as dead bodies.

"You're good."

Ricki looked up. It was the woman in the Led Zeppelin t-shirt.

"I said, you're good. You play like scrambled eggs—confusion all over. You got centipede fingers, you play so fast."

Ricki flicked ashes onto her jeans. Makes them smell funny, but they fade faster that way. "Thanks."

The woman sat down at Ricki's feet. "Those guys are terrible, even playing punk. They're out of tune, offbeat and not one could find the groove in his ass. But you are good."

Ricki looked away into the yard. Her eyes were burning from the cigarette and not having slept last night. I can't believe I couldn't sleep because of this. She shook the thought out of her head.

"You don't think so?" the woman asked, leaning against Ricki's leg.

"Think so? Baby, I know so." Ricki shifted in the lawn chair. "That isn't up for debate."

"I'm a musician, too. I'm trying to get a band together, all women." She smiled quickly, showing off a dimple. "My name is Nadine."

"Rickshaw Jones," she replied, sticking the cigarette in her mouth and offering her hand. "Nice to meet you."

Nadine stayed for the rest of the set, helped the band break down the equipment when they finished, helped Boff pick up the empty bottles and other trash littering the house and yard, then took Ricki to her apartment and helped her undress. Later, much later, Ricki sat up in bed, thinking oh, my god, what am I doing with a white girl, but Nadine wouldn't stop, wouldn't let her go, kept on till Ricki forgot she even had a question and instead floated on the electricity coming from her skin.

"How old are you?" she asked one night as they lay in Nadine's bed.

"Twenty-something," Nadine said, circling Ricki's belly button with the tips of her fingers.

Twenty-seven or eight, Ricki decided. White people don't hide their age too good.

That first week, Nadine would get out of bed humming and ready to make breakfast. The second week she'd get up to make coffee; now, she just stayed where she was smoking a cigarette.

Ricki shivered into her jeans, squirming to get them to fit right and yanked on a t-shirt. She got on her hands and knees to look under the bed. "You seen my socks?"

Nadine blew out a column of smoke. "Why don't you just move in?"

"Got no money, got no job and Liberty'd have a fit."

"Who cares what your mom thinks?"

"I care." Ricki found her socks and unrolled them. She sat on the end of the bed and rubbed the bottom of her foot. Be nice if Nadine would sweep the floor some time. "I'm already going to catch hell for coming over here instead of going to school."

"Since when does a rock star need school? What do you think of the tape I gave you?"

Ricki shrugged and jammed a foot into a hightop tennis shoe. "I really like melody. The girls in your band don't."

"You coming over to rehearse tonight?"

"I don't know." She leaned over the bed and kissed Nadine's forehead. "I don't like mixing music with other things. Causes complications."

Nadine grabbed the front of her shirt. "Yes or no?"

"I said I don't know."

She stared into Ricki's face.

"Let me go, Nadine."

Nadine loosened her grip and Ricki stood up, smoothing her shirt. She put on her other shoe and grabbed her jean jacket.

"I love you," Nadine shouted.

Ricki tore through the front door, stumbling on her unlaced shoes. She's stuck on me, sure as hell sticks to a sin, she thought, shoving her arms into her jacket while walking to the bus stop. I been sleeping with Nadine for four months, and, like that isn't enough, she wants me to go join her stupid band and sing stupid songs and I don't even think I like her. Ricki glanced down Nicollet for a bus. And she says she loves me, Ricki grinned and yanked the collar of her jacket up. Hey, it's like people singing oh, beautiful for spacious skies and linking their arms to look like the amber waves of grain: you got to expect it.

Ezekiel saw a wheel...

People talked, of course. You have to expect it, Isra thought, shifting on the couch. Rumors bounce around school like a superball and I've heard all of them. At least her other little friends never even let on what was going on, but this Nadine person arrives in her red Toyota every afternoon to pick up Ricki, some days even kissing her hello. God. Some white girl's got the hots for my sister and my sister isn't even batting an eye or trying to be normal. Ricki never has made an effort to be like other girls—playing weird music in a weird band with a bunch of druggies, growing her hair wild, she must have a need to outrage people. But it's none of my business, even though Rebecca refers to her as the Freak.

Way in the middle of the air...

Isra sighed and picked up *Romeo and Juliet* again, trying to ignore the reggae music.

"Well?" Ricki asked.

Liberty sipped her tea. "It's got a nice beat. What's that scratchy part?"

"That's not supposed to happen. The other guitar player isn't very good. Wait. Here comes my bit."

Ricki's voice soared over the jumble of instruments and filled the room.

Oh, the wheel did shine / Like God's grace falling down / Oh that wheel glowed / God's love shining down…

"You sound really good, honey. Beautiful singing."

"What do you think, Isra?"

"I don't like reggae," she answered flatly, not looking up from her script.

"You ever play any blues, Ricki?"

"Not in these bands." Ricki shrugged. "Never sounds right when I play, you know, like I'm off-rhythm or something. Yaz tries to help, but I wish some of those other old guys were around so we could jam."

There's a wheel in a wheel in a wheel…

"So do I, baby girl," she said softly. The only one who might still be living is Big Henry, and I haven't seen him since he disappeared. Used to visit every week or so, sporting a new suit and the newest haircut. God knows he had money—the used car business always pays.

Big Henry drove up on the Fourth of July in a little Italian car with three presents wrapped in shiny paper. A new leotard for Israellen.

"Purple is my first favorite color, but yellow is my second. Thank you, Big Henry." She hugged him around the neck.

"Want you to look like a pretty little daffodil when you're dancing, girl," he said.

The silk scarf was lovely and Liberty knew he'd taken a lot of time picking it out. "I don't know what I'll wear it with, but I promise you I will."

"Next time I'll bring you an evening gown to match. Then we'll go out on the town."

She kissed him on his rough cheek. "You're looking sharp."

"So are all of you." He straightened his handmade necktie, then stuck a huge hand out to Ricki. "Hey, little sister, lay on some skin."

Rickshaw slapped his palm.

"Right on, babe," he said. "You doing good in school?"

"Don't have school now. It's summer vacation."

"How was it when you did?"

"I'm learning to play the piano. I snuck into the auditorium to use theirs."

"Yeah? Billy Wayne'd be proud of you. Maybe you can learn some of this."

Another Bessie Smith album. "Thanks," she tossed over her shoulder as she raced into the living room to the hi-fi.

"Don't be playing that now, Ricki," her mother said.

"Aw, let the kid play it, Liberty Grace."

Isra rested her hand on Henry's arm and *pliéd*.

"Very nice," he whispered.

Music blasted out of the speakers.

"Turn it down, Ricki," Liberty shouted, "We know the stereo works, now turn it down."

I went down to the river / Sat beneath a willow tree...

"Ricki?" Liberty peered around the corner at her daughter. Ricki was standing as if turned to stone by the music. "Ricki?"

There were dewdrops on those willow leaves / and it rolled right down on me...

"Uh huh?"

"This is the blues, honey. Want to put something else on? How about Martha and the Vandellas?"

And that's the reason I got those weepin' willow blues...

"Don't like no Vandellas."

"You did yesterday."

Rickshaw didn't move, but kept staring at the record going around and around.

"Ricki," Henry called from the kitchen. "You heard your mama, put something else on, baby. We'll keep Bessie for special occasions."

Ricki took the record off as Liberty returned to her chair in the kitchen. The stereo blared again, this time Jimi Hendrix slashed through the house with the intro of "Are You Experienced?" screaming out, Ricki screaming along with it.

"Turn it down!" Liberty shouted.

Ricki turned down the volume.

"I hate this song," Liberty said to Henry. "She plays it over and over, not the whole album, just that one song. She's trying to learn it on her guitar."

If you can just get your mind together...

Ricki hummed the music and concentrated. The record skipped. She nudged the needle gently.

And then come on across to me...

"How old is she?" Henry asked in amazement.

"Eight. We've warped one album already."

We'll pass and then we'll watch the sunrise...

He shook his head. "She like Jimi that much?"

"Turn it down more, Ricki," Liberty called, then turned back to Henry. "That girl loves guitars. Loud, soft. And don't you worry about her quitting, she plays everyday, thanks to Terry Cee."

From the bottom of the sea...

"Terry Cee." Henry shook his head again. "Vietnam is a bad scene, getting worse and worse. Government keeps sending brothers to die in the jungle, not going to be any of us left."

But first, are you experienced?...

Henry sighed. "They're growing up quick, your twins."

"Still babies."

"You'll say that till they have children of their own."

Liberty smiled and shrugged.

Or have you ever been experienced?...

"You hear from Emma lately?" she asked.

"Three years ago I got a postcard. Said, 'Greetings from Mississippi, the Magnolia State.' On the back she wrote, 'Don't you wish you were here?' That was September 1966."

Well, I ammmmm, floated softly into the kitchen.

"That's a long time, Henry."

"I know. Too long. Delia, too. I told Emma last time she was here, that I got plenty of money now. You and Dee can come live with me, I said, we'll be a family again. But Delia's still making a living flat on her back, and Emma, well, hell. She's probably a Panther now, she's gotten so militant." Henry pulled out a cigarette and tapped it on the table, the chair squeaking under his weight. "Don't get me wrong, Liberty, I understand what Emma's trying to do, but all this violence is getting us nowhere fast. Old Loose-lips Rap Brown is going to get every black businessman shot at or fire-bombed or bankrupt." He tapped the cigarette once more, put it in his mouth and lit it.

Isra pirouetted on the smooth linoleum floor and slammed into Henry's back.

"Isra!" Liberty snapped. "If you're going to practice, you better make sure you're not going to hurt yourself or anybody else. Now, get your sister and get ready for bed."

"Liberty—"

"No arguing, prima donna. Go on."

The stereo went silent.

"Ricki, be sure to put that record away and turn on the radio."

"Okay." The radio came on.

"Thank you."

"Welcome."

"Good kids, Liberty," Henry confided. "Good looking, too, especially your little ballerina. Going to have to watch the boys around her."

"They'll know how to take care of themselves."

"Just like their mama." He leaned his elbows on the table. *Way in the middle of the air . . .*

Like I hope you can, Henry, Liberty thought, tapping her foot to the reggae. Funny how the ones who seem strongest are always the first ones to break. Liberty glanced out the window. Through the curtain sheers and the darkness of the night, she could see the outlines of trees and cars against the snow, how the neighbors' porchlights fell into oval pools of gold that looked as if they were trying to touch one another. She shivered. Just looking makes me cold now, I know I am getting old. Just looking brings back all the memories of the way things feel. Sometimes that seems more real than actually feeling anything. She sighed and stood up.

"I'm going to bed."

Ezekiel saw a wheel...

"It's not even eight o'clock," Ricki protested. "And it's only the first song."

"Long day," Liberty said, taking her tea with her. "Don't worry, baby. I'll listen to the rest of the tape later. Just leave it here for me, okay?"

Way in the middle of the air...

She kissed each of them between the eyebrows and walked back to her room. Setting the teacup onto the nightstand, she turned on the small clock radio. Glancing at the trim along the ceiling, she followed it with her eyes three-quarters of the way around the square room. White walls, blue quilt, cherry-wood dresser Emma gave me years ago, keeps amazing me how much I like this room. Just how much I like this house. I feel part of it, felt this way since I bought it. She settled into bed and snuggled into the covers. Such a good feeling—to be safe even when the bad things happen.

Bad things did happen. This was a fact. But a house made it possible to build a place of safety. To keep a place of safety. She'd defended it once, she would again.

Liberty leaned against the windowsill. At least my six-year-old twins got a safe home. The humidity and sudden cooling of the summer night knocked an ache into Liberty's leg, the one that took away her dancing days. Part-time, now full-time, push my girls off to school first thing in the morning, rush to get home before they do. My special hours, Madame says. Means they get to pay me less and fire me first. So what else is new? At least it's better than cleaning white people's dirt, as Cherise said. Need a job that will let you live independent, she told me, since you'll be working all your life, best to find work that will give you dignity, work that you can love.

The shadows of the branches lay in an undisturbed pattern on the quiet street, the porchlights shining a safe yellow under the quiet night, the other houses with their lit windows looking like fortresses against the darkness. The shiny body of a june bug sat outside the windowsill. The Sudheimers' barbecuing mixed with a sweet smell of early summer. The night was quiet, even the crickets calling to one another settled. The stars appeared not at all remote and the moon was so bright, everything she could see drew a picture of itself in sooty shadow.

Liberty eased away from the windowsill to the bed, settling back against the pillows and listening to the house shift. Even little houses shift. Even new houses sound older than the people living in them. Banfield Street was quiet except for the familiar sounds.

But that.

Breaking glass.

In front of the house. She listened intently. A branch through one of the small windows in front? No branches near enough and it's not that windy. An animal? Not cold enough to send them indoors, not in June. Besides, it was too quiet for any animal but one planning to come in.

Her scalp itched as if trying to move out of danger. She glanced at the phone next to the bed. She lifted it slowly off the hook. By the time I call, whoever it is will be gone, she realized. Another sound.

Damn, damn, damn. She hung up the phone and slowly got out of bed, knowing exactly where the creaky parts of the floor were; two babies who wouldn't sleep through the night taught her all the noise-making parts. This is my house, she thought, using both hands to lift the shotgun from behind the bedroom door, the very same gun Cherise used to shoot her no-good husband, at least that was the story. Liberty kept it as Mamie and Cher had, except for an important difference—no shells. No way she was going to have a loaded gun in her house, not with two rug-rat children getting into everything. She slid the iron bar off the triggers and disengaged the safety. If I'm going to bluff, I better do it right.

She slipped to her door and peered down the long hall to the living room. There was an outline against the wall, something big, moving, searching. Her feet cushioned like a cat's, her legs and back strong enough to move slowly and softly, she moved down the corridor, making no sound but her own breathing.

This is my house.

Mine.

She flipped the light switch on with her elbow, gun fitting tight against her shoulder.

"Move one-hundredth of one percent of an inch and you'll be left with less than one ball to play with."

The white man blinked in the light, then stared at the barrels of the gun aimed at him. With his hand he clutched a pillowcase, heavy with what he'd stolen.

My things. My house. "Don't move."

"I ain't moving, don't get nervous."

She aimed the gun a little lower, right at his inseam. "Put your hands up."

"Lady, I'm sorry."

"I said, put your hands up."

He raised his hands in the air, showing two ovals of sweat around his armpits. "I'm just trying to get some food for my kids."

"Food's in the fridge, not on the mantle where my clock used to be."

My house. I got my clock back on the mantle and threw him out. Fixed the window the next day with a sheet of glass and some putty. Never a problem since, maybe it was a charm. Liberty turned off the light and tapped the sleep button on the radio. My house, she thought, closing her eyes. This is my house.

Isra's knee ached from walking. I'll wait here, she decided, sitting on a patch of gray-green grass and staring out to sea. More laughter intertwined with the wind. On the beach below a group of people were playing rounders. Just like the chicken-base we played when we were kids. Isra glanced up. The sky was a deep blue as if layer after layer of color was heaped around the earth. There, above the arches of the ruin and the woman lying on the mountains, the first star emerged. Is there anything more beautiful than the first star? she wondered as it winked at her, sharp and white. This star knew my mother; who belonging to me will know it when I'm gone?

Four

Ricki stood at the end of the gravel path peering ahead, the sand a layer of gold from the sun, her eyes aching from too little sleep. Bad dreams don't help. When she started out on the road with the band, one kept coming back. It was as if someone was shaking the graveyard near Banfield Street and all the bodies were flying out of the ground. Then Liberty would stand there staring, her dress clotted with mud and clay.

Strange, since we had her cremated. It's not gory, not at all, but Liberty's staring can keep me awake all night. In some ways I should find comfort; makes me think she's still watching and the dream gives me the chance to watch her back.

I feel strung out. I used to be braver at night, she thought, staring out the window of the van and smoking cigarette after cigarette. She'd start smoking after a gig, when Yaz, Marcel and Malcolm would kick off their shoes and start snoring as they headed for the next town. The stink of dirty feet was enough to drive her to drink, which wasn't smart because she might have to drive, so she'd smoke to block out the smell. Staring at her own reflection in the glass, Ricki could see only a mask with the features of her mouth, the arch of cheekbones and the slope of her nose. Marcel's going to be mad in the morning when he finds out I smoked the whole pack. Smoking is stupid, anyway; shaves the edge off my high notes. One day I'll wake up to find my voice gone to ashes. But how else can I fight a ghost? All I got is smoke and staying up. How long can a woman go without sleep? Depends on the motive, I guess. A woman with job worries will last a few days, one with money troubles a little longer and a woman bothered about her children will go longer yet. But give me the chance to stay awake because of love and I'll float through my life without needing a wink.

"What beautiful hands you have," Angel whispered, kissing Ricki's fingers one by one.

The heat from her mouth spread up her wrist and beyond. Square jaw, dark, dark eyes flecked with gold from the last of the sunset coming through the windows of the loft, only Angel's mouth gives her passion away. "How do you do it?"

"Do what?"

Ricki shrugged and pulled her hands into her lap. How can you make me ache, she wanted to ask. A rush of awareness arched against all the places Angel had kissed earlier. She twined her fingers together.

"You do have beautiful hands," Angel continued, no longer whispering. "I love how they look. I love how they taste. I love the way they touch me. Mostly I love the music you play with them."

Ricki's fingers went tighter yet.

"That music. It's the best expression of you. Makes sense that your hands should be so beautiful."

Ricki glanced at the stacked dishes on the table, then back to Angel, now sketching on a napkin.

"I had a lover who was a sculptor. He had the ugliest hands I've ever seen. The backs were covered with hair, his fingers were short and stubby, reminded me of those white long-capped mushrooms. Had a dick like one, too. But he was a good sculptor. Maybe even great. Let me see your hand again."

She raised her hand to the table. "My sister has beautiful hands. She's very graceful. She always has been. I think that's why ballet fit her so well, you know, she's always been like that. Me and dancing never got along too well—I quit when I was eight and too big to be harmless any more." "Harmless? Bet you've been a pushover all your life. Rough, tough Ricki Jones, genius musician." Angel pushed over the sketch. "I even signed it. Put it in your pocket." Ricki looked at the drawing. It was her hand, even the tattered rope bracelet was there falling over her wrist. "Pretty good." "Ought to be. I been doing art all my life. I'm my own best creation."

Why didn't I see it, why didn't I get it from the beginning that Angel's exactly what she looks like? Not like some of us. Ricki smiled, the mask of white reflected in the window grimacing back. The landscape was flat as far as she could see, the lights on the highway shining just over the shoulder of the road and that was all. At least Angel pointed the way to the blues by way of a broken heart. Should feel obliged to her for that.

Ricki shifted in the seat, the vinyl creaking. Donnie, the driver, was a perfect silhouette in the front of the van. Good old Donnie, nice man though the speed has burnt most of his brain cells. He and Mal and Marcel and Yaz, they've become family but I'd leave them all in a minute if Angel were to come for me. I'd leave everything like I did when she went away. Left everything but my music. I got my music as much as I got my skin and my beautiful hands. Left my sister, let her go like I didn't know her anymore. Left Liberty and didn't say a thing, just left her alone.

Tina Turner crooned a meow and jumped into Liberty's lap. You got the lonesome blues, too, cat? she thought, scratching the cat's bright white chin. You'll find them here tonight. Sitting so still but for the movement of her fingers, Liberty could feel her own heart beating, the sensation as faded as the gray haze of the sky. The sun wasn't up yet and Liberty felt so tired she hurt. In her hand was Israellen's letter from February.

Happy Valentine's Day, she had written. And Happy Valentine's Day to you, too, I thought. You've finally gotten around to writing to your mama, though it's not much of a letter. The paper is so light, like dust on my fingers; I'm surprised it could carry much of anything, much less a heavy biblical name like Caleb. How could a fragile letter come all the way across the ocean carrying a name like that?

Liberty dropped the letter on the end table. The loneliness has been touchable this winter—the past couple weeks especially, since Isra arrived—and colder than ever. The season is dragging on me, working muscles I didn't even know a human body had. I'm still cold, heating bill's outrageous, and I can't seem to get warm. It must be my empty house and being tired. I'm just tired. Thank god I've got only one more day of teaching till the weekend, then I can catch up on my sleep.

She sighed. Why did I ever have children? So I wouldn't be alone? Did I have so much hope for the world or did it happen because I wasn't thinking, just wanted to mix myself with Will and come out whole and my girls were what was left over? Or did I do it because I can be alone, I know how to be alone. You got to know how to do that because children leave you lonelier than any lover can. And I thought I could live without my children.

But now my little girls are gone. I wanted to think Isra going away wouldn't make any difference. She'd always be the prima donna. But I see that's not true and I'm caught between loss and letting go. I'm willing to open my hands, release them into their own lives, but I didn't expect it to make them strangers. Not strangers to me and certainly not strangers to each other. Ricki on the road and Isra on the other side of the world. I never thought they'd get so far away.

Liberty leaned over the big crib. Beautiful two-year-olds. They hold hands when they sleep. Perfect, every part of their small selves: their eyes, their mouths, their legs and little hands. How much I want to protect them, yank the hurt in life away as I would a book of matches from their hands. My god, I think this living business is just too much for me. She glanced at their fingers, noticing the half-moon along the backs of their nails, hazy as if drawn in chalk. I want my arms to be as strong as my children believe they are.

"Morning," Ricki said.

"Morning, baby," she said back, her voice almost too soft to be heard. It hurt to talk, as if somewhere deep in her, her spirit had taken the pain from the news she just heard, each name a blow. Addie May Collins. Denise McNair. Carole Robertson. Cynthia Welsley. Four little girls in their Sunday dresses. Four little girls blown to bits at the 16th Street Baptist Church. Liberty had turned on the radio near her bed, smacking the top as it screeched static. It was the radio from Cherise and Mamie's bedroom, and back then it'd only picked up the CBS network, fading out when Edward R. Murrow came on the air. Mamie had said the radio was an anarchist and that was the only way it could object to the war in Europe and the way white bands massacred Negro music. Billy Wayne said he fixed it, which meant he opened the back, peered at its dirty old insides while mumbling to himself. Liberty smacked it again and got the latest news of hate and disaster.

"Pancakes for breakfast?" Isra asked, crawling out of bed.

Liberty laid her hand onto her daughter's small head. Those little girls. Their mothers, she knew, will forget and cook too much. They'll glance out the window, expecting a daughter to come up the porch and in the door, hungry and needing a wash. Now all of us will spend our time with one eye looking out the window, watching for slow-moving cars with white insides.

Two months later Kennedy was killed and Liberty got a letter from Emma that said a peckerwood sheriff holding her and twelve others declared a national holiday and served them fried chicken from his own table. Liberty looked over the sheet of paper covered with Emma's scrawl at her two daughters. Someday trouble will ring the doorbell asking for them. What will I do then? Liberty smiled bitterly, folding the worn letter.

That night, after putting her children to bed, pausing only to hold their faces in her hands after kissing them goodnight, Liberty took down a bottle of Smithe's Patent Leather and Patina Cleaner, a handful of cotton balls and two pairs of small, shiny tap shoes from the top shelf of the closet near the front door. Their first pairs. Christmas presents. Bought almost brand new. Liberty'd gotten her first pair when she was eight from Ollie, a funny-looking white boy with gray skin from not enough sun. When he heard Liberty was going to learn to dance he set them next to the *Pioneer Press* he delivered that morning. Poor Ollie. His mom wore two different shoes when she went outside, and Liberty'd see him, eyes glued to her feet and not saying a thing to hurt her feelings. They locked his mother up for good after the winter she caught pneumonia from running around outdoors wearing only her nightgown. Ollie quit his paper route and took care of all six kids, making sure they got to school and didn't do anything their father would remember when he drank himself to violence every Saturday night.

In the kitchen, Liberty sat at the table shining the twins' shoes as night spun slowly into day. Outside, a wind blew so cold it felt like needles and the luminescent night-sky promised snow.

That was Rondo, she thought, scratching the cat's ears. Black or white, if you were on the fringe like us, you looked out for one another. Ollie was on the fringe. Old Annie was on the fringe. Having somebody to look out for, that's an important thing, as important as having somebody look out for you. Liberty glanced out the window. Hard frost, unusual in March, etched the glass into a Christmas card, all lace and crystal.

Isra wanting to get married, she says. Caleb, what sort of name is that? I've had two weeks of listening to it—his name isn't very long away from Isra—and it still doesn't fit in my mouth. Sounds like it came out of the Bible when it should've stayed there. She wants to marry him and I can't even say the boy's name. That's a sign if I was one to believe in signs. Since when has marriage done anyone any good? If she wants children, she should just have children and hope her man is decent enough not to bother her afterwards. Like Will. My William. He's mine in a way weddings and honeymoons can never touch. And Will understood.

"It's been a while," she'd said simply.

"Ten years."

"Lost track of you."

Will sat carefully on the sofa, not even taking off his jacket. Liberty had known him as a man whose hands never shook, but now he clutched them tightly around a can of Old Milwaukee. His pants were only thread in some places and too big. Much too big. There was a reedy tremor in his voice and his pale skin, which burned so easily during those long hot days on the road, was almost transparent, as if the blood vessels were retreating deeper and deeper and taking all their color with them. He looks so old, she thought, so old and thin.

"How are the kids?" he asked.

"How did you hear of them?"

"Emma. They were born on October fourteenth, 1960, she said, Israellen and Rickshaw Jones. Besides," he glanced around the room. "Looks like kids live here."

"So you found Emma?"

"Years ago."

"She never told me."

"She spent a day, day and a half in Georgia, passing through."

Like always, Liberty thought. She was always a ghost before she became one. "The kids are fine. At school right now."

"Doing okay?"

"They're doing all right."

He stared at his beer can. "I never was very good in school. Always getting yelled at, ran away when I was twelve. Think they'll go to college?"

"Lord, let me live through fourth grade, then I'll start thinking about it. Right now, Isra wants to be a ballerina and Ricki wants music."

"Yeah?" he grinned again and looked at his shoes. "That fits, doesn't it?"

"Maybe, maybe."

He drank some more of his beer. "Wish I could see them kids, Liberty."

"Isra has dance after school, be home by five-thirty. Ricki said she was going along to watch, though what she says and what she does are not necessarily connected. They'll be home by dinnertime."

"Wouldn't be right, me just showing up."

"People do it all the time here. More like a magician's hat than a house with all the appearing and disappearing."

"Seen some of the old folks?"

"You heard Billy Wayne died? Diabetes, heart attack, everything and anything. And his boy, Terry Cee..." she trailed off. Her throat hurt suddenly just with the thought of telling. All those lives. But their dying doesn't take them away, not really.

"I heard about Emma."

She nodded again and sipped her beer.

"I'm sorry, Liberty."

"So am I."

And Emma Nevada's not gone either, not really. Emma, Cherise, all of them are in the sky, constellations I made my very self. Every clear night their light shines down on me.

"Really wish I could see those kids," he said again. "But I can't. Time I started rolling on."

They both smiled in remembrance. Roll on: the truck packed, everybody ready, and Will and Liberty up front leading the way. Like mailmen, she thought, through sleet and snow and rain and dead of night, we kept on pushing our luck till it broke. Liberty studied his face. Pain was unhidden now, as if every year that passed loosened the mask over his true face like wild flowers do the pavement. Just looking at him made her feel older, not in a dried-up, broken way, but in a way that could build mountains.

"I just dropped by for a hello. No, don't get up, wait here,

124

just for a minute." He shuffled through his bag for a small box with a huge red bow that he set on her lap. "For you and the old days and the new days. Say hi to those twins for me."

She stared at the box till she could no longer hear his car. The ribbon and bow slid off easily because she knew he would've asked the clerk not to tape it down since it would ruin the shine and what was the use of getting something pretty if it was ruined? The tissue paper crushed in her hand like a fistful of butterflies. Chocolate-covered cherries. Just like always. With the cellophane wrapper off. The first time he'd given her a box of chocolate-covered cherries, she'd found a small square note in his crooked handwriting that was unreadable and she had to go to him for translation. He went red all the way to his ears when he read the love poem to her. Liberty didn't speak to Will for three days, till they hit Florida and she had to sit up front with him because she was so light, she'd pass for Mexican if no one looked too hard and white people would leave them alone thinking they were migrant workers.

On top of the candy was an envelope. It was cream-colored and thick, more than a note. She popped one of the candies into her mouth. Even the oldest unused habits never die, she thought as the syrup filled her mouth and the sweetness made two teeth twinge. The box went back to the table, the lid back on because Tina Turner liked chocolate, and she examined the envelope. Liberty looked inside. A bank book. A letter.

Dear Liberty,

A man at the bank is writing this letter for me. His name is Mr. James Robinson. If you go to him with the bank book, you will find some money from the sale of the farm in an account for you and the twins. Mr. Robinson promised to handle all the details for you as soon as you contact him.

I love you still.

Will Ross

The first time Will said he loved me, I remember it as clearly as ever, his t-shirt was so white and ribbed with his bones and muscles. You don't know me, I laughed, you don't know me. What a fool, as if any human being got to know another even after years and years.

Liberty ran her fingers through the cat's soft fur. Happy Valentine's Day, Isra wrote. She was right, it was Valentine's. All the heart-shaped boxes were out for display, every florist advertising roses and my ballerina said she was coming home to visit for two weeks. I remember she left just before the leaves were off the trees. I remember the maple out front looked like a tongue of fire in my front yard. Big Henry said I'd regret planting that tree, its roots were sure to interfere with the underground pipes.

Liberty turned away from the maple tree, its leaves burning with color. "You'll be careful, Isra?"

"Yes, Liberty."

"You'll write?"

"Yes."

The taxi driver closed the trunk and got into the driver's seat.

"The airport please," Isra said.

Liberty slammed the door shut and stepped onto the sidewalk. She waved once as the cab pulled away.

Isra waved back over her shoulder. That shack won't ever hold me again, she decided. Hello, London, here I come. Excitement made her stomach twinge. I've never even been on an airplane and I'm going to fly across the Atlantic Ocean. This is one dream that's going to come true, she thought. I'm going to London!

"I'm a dancer, Durben. I'm not an actor. I don't even know if I want to be an actor. I tried out because I want to be onstage. But I'm a ballet dancer, it's all I've ever wanted to be."

The teacher smiled. "Sometimes we don't get to pick what we're going to be."

"That's not what Liberty says."

"Maybe you're not supposed to be a ballerina. Maybe your dancing was to give you the ability to be whatever you want. You know how to set your mind. All that discipline you have, that's worth something. Now, I don't know much about ballet, but I know some injuries can finish a career before it's begun, like yours. But you didn't hurt your mind. You didn't hurt your greatest ability. You have enough discipline to be a brain surgeon if you so decided."

I want to be a dancer, Isra thought.

"And you're good enough to make it. When you walk onstage, Israellen, everything shifts in your direction. But you need to train somewhere, someplace that will do you justice, and you need to make up your mind. It's a lot of work to take on with only half a heart."

Isra said nothing.

"Why are you so afraid?"

Why am I afraid? Isra flopped over on the sofa, the script flat on the floor. Being onstage? Failing? Succeeding? Just because I love ballet doesn't mean I can't be an actor. Durben said dramatic characters are never allowed to move towards their goals unimpeded. Why do I get the feeling that the same is happening to me?

The front door banged open. Rickshaw dragged in, guitar case in one hand, the other hand pressing a bloody napkin against her forehead.

Isra jumped from the couch, her knee twinging. "What in the hell happened?"

"Got hit by a bottle."

"Let me see it, put your hand down. Hold your hair back, I don't know why you wear it like that anyway, all those knots. It's so ugly. Oh my god, you're bleeding all over the place. We got to clean it up."

She led Ricki into the bathroom. Ricki sat down on the edge of the bathtub, still holding her guitar. Opening the medicine cabinet, Isra grabbed the cotton and Merthiolate.

"You going to tell me what happened?" she asked, carefully washing the blood away.

"No."

Isra shrugged. "This is going to sting."

"Yeow!" Rickshaw jumped.

"Sit still," Isra commanded.

"It hurts. Did you get the part?"

"Yeah. You need a bandage," she said, rummaging through the medicine cabinet.

"You going to be the star?"

"One of them." Isra pulled out some gauze and surgical tape and carefully cut a bandage. "Doesn't look too deep, but any injury to your head could be fatal. It might let all the air out."

"You're quite a comedian, baby sister."

Israellen taped the bandage firmly on her sister's forehead. "There. Maybe I'll be a brain surgeon when I grow up."

"If you grow up." Ricki looked in the mirror. "Great. I look like a lobotomy patient."

"What happened?"

"Somebody threw a bottle."

"Why didn't you duck?"

Ricki stepped out of the bathroom and into her bedroom. "I thought I did."

"Uh huh. Who threw it?"

"I don't know. Hope I didn't bleed on my guitar." Ricki set her guitar case on her bed and opened it. "Looks okay. What's the name of the play?"

"*The Effect of Gamma Rays on Man-in-the-Moon Marigolds.*"

"It any good?"

"Won a Pulitzer. That's like the Grammies of writing."

"Who do you play?"

"I'm Ruth. She's in high school and kind of weird."

"You won't have a problem with the weird part. Is she black?"

"Why?"

"She ain't, huh? Well, good luck being a white girl, that will take some acting. Guess I shouldn't worry—you've had plenty of experience." Ricki leaned her guitar against the wall.

Isra pulled herself up to her full height and deflected her anger. "It's a very challenging part. With a professional company. Want to help me with my lines?"

"Naw." Ricki shrugged out of her jean jacket. I got to get my amp and call my girlfriend. Angel, baby. She held up the leather jacket Angel lent her. "Think it's too hot for this?"

"No."

Ricki pulled it on and started down the hall.

"I've been talking to Durben," Isra called after her, trying to get her sister's attention.

"Yeah? How is that old bag?"

"She's not an old bag. She thinks I should go to London."

"Ain't you good enough for America?"

"To the Royal Academy of Dramatic Arts. It's the best place to study acting, Ricki."

"How should I know that kind of shit, baby sister?" Ricki gave her a crazy grin and walked out of the house. Her stomach started to tighten up as if a bolt of speed was racing around her muscles, lacing them tight in anticipation of Angel. Then we get loose all over the place, lord, what a woman, she thought. I swear since that night trouble just slides off like water on a duck's back. Meeting Angel. My Angel. My lover. What did I do to meet such a gal?

Ricki let out a James Brown howl that ended in a Little Richard hiccup. She tried a Janis Joplin shriek that almost made her throat collapse, wavered in and out of a Rick James falsetto, then backed the song down the scale, ending it. No applause, not on a weeknight. She stepped over the stage lights kept in place by duct tape and made her way to the bar, counting the heaps of clothing with drinks in front of them.

"You're sounding good, sugar," Johnny said, putting a glass up on the bar for her. "Like always."

She climbed up on a stool and tapped her knuckles against

the mahogany, the only sound in the place. "You seen Yaz?"

"He'll show up. Always does when he wants a drink." Johnny himself was once a musician, played bass till he busted his left hand boxing Golden Gloves, he told Ricki the first night she worked here over a year ago. Would've won the fight, too, but lost his power punch and his chance to fight the number one contender. Missed out on jamming with the hottest jump band on the chittlin' circuit, too. Johnny noticed a hand waving at the other end of the bar. "Drink your soda, I'll be back."

Rickshaw leaned on her elbow and sipped her Bubble-Up. He won't even stick in a dash of whiskey for taste, says I got to keep steady. Geez. She sighed and reached over the bar for one of Johnny's cigarettes.

"Hey," he shouted.

She dropped them and sat back down. I'm almost twenty-one years old, for god's sake.

"Cigarette?" someone asked.

Ricki turned her head.

"Have one," the woman said, holding out a pack.

Ricki slid one out and the woman lit it. "Thanks."

"You're welcome." The woman sat on the stool next to Ricki and signaled the bartender. Her hair was almost shoulder length, straight and black, framing her angular face. Mexican, Ricki thought, Cuban, Puerto Rican, maybe, but no accent and three sheets or more to the wind. No older than me and good looking, she decided, trying to get a glance at the rest of her, but the dark didn't give away any secrets. If the rest of her matches what I see, she's got to be hot. Johnny set a shot in front of the woman.

"You want a drink?" she asked Ricki.

"Got one."

"How old are you?"

"Too young for you to be messing with," Johnny butted in suddenly, staring at the woman. His mouth was open a little and his jaw squared, like he was waiting for a fight. A drunken voice called and he walked away, his shoulder twitching.

"You make friends easy," Ricki said.

"He doesn't like my kind," she said, slapping back the shot.

"What kind is that?"

"The entertaining kind. Are you done for the night?"

Ricki glanced around the bar. "Pretty much, since nobody's come down to jam."

"Let's go," she said, sliding off her bar stool.

"Where?"

"Come on."

"I have to get my guitar."

"Suit yourself," she threw over her shoulder.

"What's your name?"

The woman turned to face her. Her eyes gleamed like the light on the bell of a horn. "Angel."

Angel tossed Ricki the keys to her car, rattled off an address and slumped into the passenger seat of her Fiat. When Ricki pulled over in front of a huge dark warehouse, Angel opened her door and stumbled out of the car.

"This way," she said.

The freight elevator squeaked in a way that made Ricki want to squeeze her fist so tight, her nails would go through the back of her hands. She followed Angel down a narrow hallway, the darkness punctuated with a single light bulb. The floors were plywood and sounded hollow. Giving me the creeps in here, Ricki thought, looking around. One wall was white, broken only with doors, posters and streaks of dirt. Small factory windows stretching twenty feet to the ceiling interrupted with vents and pipes made up the outer wall. It was quiet but for their footsteps.

"Home again, home again," Angel murmured, taking the keys and unlocking the door.

Ricki walked in. A long high row of the same windows made up a whole corner, and Minneapolis spread out before them. Dim track lights flicked on, beaming at a series of huge sketches hanging almost to the ceiling on the one plain white wall. Another light shone on the wood stairs that led up to a loft along the back wall.

"My studio," Angel said simply, setting Ricki's guitar against the wall, then leading her upstairs by the hand.

The next afternoon, Ricki untangled herself from the sheets and Angel's body. Sun lit up the loft. She walked naked to the bathroom in the other corner, trying not to waken Angel, feeling strange with the windows revealing her to the city below. Getting into the shower intensified the feeling of exposure, but she shut her eyes and forgot about the city as the warm water cascaded over her. New memories flooded against her skin, sinking deeper than the water ever could.

Nadine. Tayla. Jackie. Ricki closed her eyes and counted them, her other lovers. Max. Jinna. A white girl, four black girls and now this one. Each one better than the last, she thought, remembering how they sound and undress and move. I remember each as if seeing them under a bright light. But this one—how to compare living, breathing Angel with them. That's how it is, that's how it's going to be—Angel and the others, not even all of them can get close to this one. This one is different. Magically, incredibly different. Maybe it was the little bit of her dope they smoked, though Ricki had smoked dope and had sex before—it only made everything funnier.

It's Angel.

"Christ!"

Angel, awake and wearing a long plaid shirt, pushed the water nozzle against the wall, washing Minneapolis into a painting. As they stood, Ricki could see how they would look from the other side of the window—two hazy colors mixing into one.

"So what's your name, anyway?" Angel asked.

Ricki turned off the water. "Why do you want to know? It's only a one-nighter, ain't it?"

"Could be, except it's afternoon. Tell me."

"Ricki Jones."

"And Ricki Jones, what do you do other than play guitar and pick up strange women in low-life bars?"

"Nothing."

"Really? Most dykes I know are into at least three other things than what they're doing at the time, unless of course, they're into someone else," she cackled, stepping out of the shower. "You hungry?"

I'm starving. "What you making?"

"What am I making?" Angel walked into the kitchen leaving a trail of wet footprints on the wood and opened the small refrigerator.

Ricki watched her as she dried off. In the sunlight, her legs were tan and muscular, drops of water slipping down her skin like liquid gold.

Angel turned around. "Scrambled eggs?"

"Great," Ricki answered.

"You can wear that robe if you want."

"Thanks." She stared at the toothbrushes hanging over the sink. "Can I use one of these?"

"Sure. Not the red one. I used it for a painting. I keep it for people who are lousy in the sack."

Ricki hoped Angel didn't see her flush as she squeezed toothpaste onto the blue toothbrush.

Angel set her fork down, leaving half her breakfast. "So, are you into motorcycles? Cars? Sailboats?"

Ricki shook her head and took another bite of toast.

"Politics?"

Another shake of Ricki's head as she swallowed.

"Astrology? Palm reading? Tarot cards?"

"I stayed up one night to play poker with a deck of Tarot cards. Got a full house and three people died."

"Clever."

"I play music. I'm into guitars. What about you?"

Angel unfolded her arms, gesturing at the studio. "Right now I'm a painter."

Ricki pointed with her coffee cup at the sketches hung along the length of the studio. "What are those pictures of?"

"Characters from *Through the Looking Glass*. Have you read it?"

"No."

"Imagine being able to walk through a mirror to another world. A world that's a dream, the Red King's dream." Angel got up from the table, picked up a bottle of tequila and poured herself a glass.

Ricki walked down the steps, stopping in front of the easel. "What's this?" she asked, turning to Angel.

She followed down the stairs. "You never read *Alice in Wonderland* either, did you?"

"I don't read much."

"They made it into a movie a couple of times. The first one flopped because all the stars wore masks and no one could recognize them. Couldn't see the fucking stars, can you believe it? All you have to do is look up at the sky to see the stars."

Ricki turned back to the painting. The colors seemed to glow, making their shapes jostle against one another. And it was big, the top standing at least two feet higher than her head and resting on an easel ledge that was spattered with paint. Ricki reached out her hand and ran her finger along the wood. Dry.

"The painting's wet," Angel said gently. "You can touch it if you want."

Ricki gently rubbed a startling yellow. Slippery, greasy, she thought, suddenly aware of a scent. She pulled her hand away and sniffed the color now gilding her finger.

"Linseed oil. And me, I think. Do you like it?"

"I don't know." I like the you part, she thought, touching the painting again, her whole hand flat against a beautiful swirl of gray and blue. She stared at her palm. Looks like sun breaking through clouds.

"Beautiful," Angel whispered. She kissed Ricki lightly on the neck, where a bite from the night before was becoming a purple bruise. She reached for the tubes of paint. "We should cover that. Let's see. Burnt Umber. Prussian Blue. Teal. Here: Skin Tone. Funny, isn't it? My skin's not this color and neither is yours." With that, Angel spread a patch on Ricki's neck where she had kissed her. "Too pink."

It was that scent Ricki couldn't get rid of. Secret, hot, it was oily like tequila and sex together, so different from the sweet green smell of spring that filled Ricki's mouth as she walked up to the door on Banfield Street. Even outdoors in the late afternoon sun, she'd been unable to shake from her skin the feeling of Angel's body moving with hers. She sighed, picking up the mail. Bills, junk, no fan mail, she thought, slamming the door shut and walking into the kitchen.

"Hey, hey, Liberty Grace, what's shaking, mama?"

"You are. Better start wearing a bra or your tits'll be hanging to your knees by the time you're twenty-five."

"I'll be a star by then and nobody will care. Anything to eat?"

Liberty pointed at the refrigerator with her elbow since she was doing the dishes. "Sliced ham in there."

She pulled out the ham, mayo and two slices of bread. Damn, still have paint on my fingernails.

Liberty sniffed suddenly. "What's that smell? Something going bad in the refrigerator?"

Back in her room, Ricki yanked off her jacket and plopped on the bed, noticing her nipples standing at attention and looking for action. What a workout that woman gave me. I feel like a jigsaw puzzle just finding its last piece. Ricki squeezed her eyes shut, the memory of Angel making her skin burn. Who needs to go anywhere once she's found heaven?

Isra leaned against the cab seat. Ricki probably doesn't even know what England is. She glanced out the window. It was October, the leaves had reached their full color. Leaves only get a moment of their own, she thought, as if the trees are too jealous of them stealing the show. Soon the limbs would be-

135

come dark gray grooves like burned bones and the branches the color of doubt. A shapeless color cutting against a colorless sky. At the corner of Banfield and Forty-ninth, she glanced back. Liberty was standing where the cab had been, shielding her eyes from the autumn sun. Thank you, Liberty. Thank you.

"Thanks, Mama," Isra said, turning the envelope over in her hands and trying not to sound too disappointed.

"Really extended yourself shopping this year, didn't you?" Ricki kidded, picking hers up.

"Just open them."

Isra tore hers open and the savings account book fell into her lap.

"The money is from your daddy and from me. We both been saving since you were born. Whatever you want to do, you can do it now."

"But—"

"No buts, Rickshaw. No questions. He wanted you to use it however you wanted. I want you to do the same."

Lord, please don't get into anything that you can't handle, Israellen. Liberty watched the cab turn the corner and walked back into the house. She's gone, Israellen's gone now for sure. She didn't even want me to go to the airport with her. Inside, the house was dim after the autumn sunshine and quieter than it had ever been. "It's just you and me now, Tina Turner," Liberty said crossing her arms to hug in some lost warmth, "Just us."

An ache brushed inside her chest, like the wings of a great bird opening in her heart. A cup of tea will ease it. She walked out to the kitchen, where Isra's coffee cup sat on the table. It warmed Liberty's hand as she carried it to the sink. Didn't even finish, she thought, pouring the coffee slowly down the drain. What a beautiful color coffee is. When it's in a cup it's the color of Emma's eyes and when I pour it out it's the color of the inside of her arms.

Turning on the kettle, she walked to the refrigerator and

pulled out a half-pint of cream. "A treat," she said to the cat, "for both of us."

She poured some into a shallow bowl and set it on the floor. Tina Turner sniffed at it, then looked up at her.

"Ungrateful. You are ungrateful. I should've made Rickshaw take you to the pound." She leaned over, the bird in her chest flapping quickly from the sudden movement. With one hand she rubbed over her heart to loosen the sudden ache, and with the other, scratched the cat's neck. I could've killed that girl, honest to god. I really could have, bringing a cat into my house.

It had been February. The twins could destroy anything in record time and already their Christmas presents were frayed with abuse. A stuffed cat named Bernice was drowned in the toilet when they were playing pirates one morning. The clown marionette with wooden legs and soft, spongy body had its strings ripped out, then its head knocked off after several tries with the beanbags, which split and leaked dried peas all over the basement.

Ricki was showing Isra the attic door in the front closet when the doorbell rang.

"Get down, quick!" she whispered, both knowing they weren't supposed to be playing upstairs.

Liberty, in a terrible mood because she'd spent the morning working on her taxes, heard their voices. She yanked open the closet door. "Get out of there."

They tumbled out with one of Liberty's old winter boots. Ricki kicked it back inside as the bell rang again. Liberty opened the front door.

"Hello, Emma," she said, ignoring the icy air streaming inside.

Staring straight ahead, Emma Nevada walked into the living room. She's got to be cold, Isra thought, maybe her neck is froze so she can't look around the room. It looked better now since the three of them painted it last fall.

"It's over now, I got to get out and stay out." Emma spoke

after a long moment, the snow stretched from her shoulder to her hem melting and the water rolling down the man's survival parka she was wearing.

"Take these and put them in Isra's room." Liberty handed Emma's backpack and guitar to the twins, who raced off with them. "Let me take your coat, Emma," she said softly, pulling it off her shoulders.

Emma slept for two days straight. Ricki, who was the first home since she didn't take dance anymore, could hear her moaning as she lay dreaming in Isra's room. She knocked on the door once, twice. She could hear the bedsprings creaking and a hoarse voice call out, "Who's there?"

Ricki opened the bedroom door and walked in slowly. She was carrying a plate with two pieces of peanut butter and grape jelly toast and didn't want to drop anything.

Emma was squashed into Israellen's bed. That's weird, Ricki thought. Liberty's got a huge bed that could fit them both. She stepped around the plates on the floor.

"Here," she said, handing the plate to Emma. "I brought you something to eat."

On the third day, today, Emma stayed awake to eat. "You're a good cook," she said, dried tears looking like snail tracks from the corners of her eyes.

"Thanks." Ricki stacked all the other dishes around the bed and took them out to the sink. Sitting on the kitchen table was a small stack of school books. Her homework. She hated it. She didn't understand any of it. No matter how hard she tried, Mrs. Guardling bled all over her papers with red ink. Next week they had oral reports, and Ricki didn't know what to do. She glanced at a page. It just looked all scrambled, like somebody threw a bunch of alphabet cookies in a box and shook them up and now expected a nine-year-old to read them without any help. Sure.

Maybe she could find a record at the library to help. Ricki closed the book and pulled on her winter boots. She struggled into her coat and wrapped a scarf around her face, even though she hated the scratchy feeling against her cheeks. She liked the small hat; it was black and wool and sat in a little circle on the top of her head.

She hummed as she walked through the Sudheimers' yard and into the vacant lot. New snow dusted the fort Fat Huey's brother Ted and the Dropik boys built. It's cold. It smells good, like fires in fireplaces. Her humming twisted into "I Heard It Through the Grapevine," and slid into "You Can't Hurry Love." She made a high clicking sound and started mimicking the horn arrangement of "Rock Me, Baby," copying the B. B. King guitar breaks and almost running out of breath. That reminds me of Liberty's Johnny Ace song, she thought, kicking a pile of snow. That song she dances to in the living room when she thinks we're asleep. Ricki put her arms out and spun in a slow pirouette, her boots squeaking against the snow, then started imitating Ella Fitzgerald scat singing. That's what I am, I'm a little Ella Fitzgerald. An Ella Fitzgerald Junior with a guitar.

There were some fresh rabbit prints by the abandoned car, at least she thought they were fresh. Bet the rabbits are cold, especially their feet. Wonder where everybody is. She kicked at one of the bread crusts she, Isra and Huey had thrown out for the birds a couple of days ago, then walked across the lot. Fat Huey lived on the other side of the scrawny bushes, now heavy with snow and humped over like a line of dwarves wearing pillows. Sometimes stuff was hidden in there, like a bottle of wine and once there was a dirty magazine. Brad Dropik said he'd let her look at it if she showed her butt to him.

Ricki smacked at a bush, the snow cascading off of it, then stopped suddenly. What was that? She listened again. There it was again, right under this bush. Bet it's a rabbit, she thought, a lost baby rabbit. Down on her hands and knees, she searched under the branches. She dug away the snow heaped at the bottom, and down by the roots, in a small hollow, she saw it. That's pretty smart, she decided, that's where I'd go. She dug away enough for her arm and reached for the small squashed heap of fur crying softly.

"It's okay, it's okay," she whispered, unzipping her jacket and stuffing the kitten inside. "It's okay, cat, don't pee on me, we'll be home in a second."

Cradling the small animal against her, she ran as fast as she could in her boots. She could feel the kitten shivering through her sweater. Back at the house on Banfield Street, she slammed open the back door, pulled off her mittens, then unhooked the fur ball from her front and set it on the table.

"Stay there," she said, the cat mewing. She pulled a bowl from the cupboard, filled it with milk and set it on the table. "Drink that."

The kitten lapped away noisily as Ricki took off her outdoor clothes. She tossed her cap onto the heap of her jacket and boots, then lifted up the kitten and ran into the back room.

"Emma?" she whispered urgently walking into the room.

Emma sat up slowly.

"Guess what I got," Ricki held up the cat. "Isn't he pretty?"

Emma slid on her glasses. "Let me see, Ricki," she said, holding out her hands. Soon they were filled with a purring bundle of fuzz. "Where did you get him?"

"Found him under a bush in the vacant lot."

"Outside? He's just a baby. And," she studied the kitten, "he's not a he; he's a she."

"That's even better because we're all shes, too." Ricki plopped onto the bed beside her. "Think Liberty'll let us keep her?"

"I don't know, darling. But she's going to need food and a box, no matter what."

"There's a box downstairs."

"I mean a catbox, someplace for her to do her business in."

"A place to shit, huh?"

"Right. Well," she handed the cat back to Ricki and kicked off the blankets, "Guess we can walk to the store as well as anybody else can."

Emma found her overalls, a flannel shirt and a sweater, then pulled off her nightgown. With every move her back and arm muscles changed, the shapes clear under her skin. She was big, but so thin her ribs jutted out like a hoop of sticks around her middle. Ricki snuck a peak at her front. Her nipples were almost purple, and Emma had hair under her arms. Ricki petted the kitten's head and it began purring.

"Geez, that kitten's awful loud for such a little thing, ain't she?" Emma snapped her bibs.

You got a cute nose, little cat. "Think we should leave her here?"

"She'll be okay. Put her in a box with a little blanket for her to curl up with. Go on, now."

Ricki carried the kitten into her room and set her on the bed. As the kitten yawned and flopped onto the cover, Ricki dumped all the junk out of her toybox, kicking the toys under her bed. She stuffed in a pillow and what was left of the headless clown puppet. With both hands, she set the ball of fur inside. The kitten let out a small meow and looked up at Ricki. You trust me, don't you? Ricki thought, smoothing back the fluffy fur sticking up on the cat's head. "There you go," she said, giving her one last pet. She feels just like silk, just like the way silk ought to feel.

Emma was standing in the door. "You ready?"

When they got back, Emma made a little catbox down in the basement, using a plastic bag and a pail, filling it with the litter while Ricki got the kitten. "It'll do for now. We'll have to get a real one if Liberty lets us keep her."

The gray and white kitten dug at the litter delicately with one paw then looked up at them. Her eyes and ears are so big and the rest of her so little, it's a good thing I saved her, Ricki decided, as the kitten balanced against the edge of the box. "Liberty will let us keep her, won't she?"

"I really don't know, Rickshaw, I'm telling you the truth." Emma reached over to pet the little white spot on the kitten's nose. "Thought of a name for her yet?"

Ricki shook her head. "She should have a good name. What would be good for a gray cat?"

"Do you want to name her for somebody or for the way she looks or what?"

"I don't know, long as it's good."

Upstairs, the back door opened and slammed shut. "Ricki?" Liberty called. "Are you down there?"

"They're home," she said to Emma.

"Yep."

"Think we should take the kitten upstairs?"

"Well," Emma considered. "Liberty'd get right to the point."

Ricki nodded. She scooped up the cat and the three of them headed upstairs.

"Hello, Emma. Good to see you up," Liberty said, unwinding her scarf. "Hello, Ricki. How long has that cat been in the house?"

"An hour," Ricki answered, cradling the kitten closer.

"It's so cute, can I hold it?" Isra squealed, taking her out of Ricki's arms.

"Rickshaw Jones, how many times have I told you not to bring animals inside this house?"

Ricki didn't answer.

"And you brought it in even after I told you not to."

Isra snuggled the cat closer. "Look, it likes me. It's licking my chin. Its tongue feels funny, all rough."

"She was freezing," Ricki said suddenly. "And hungry. She was crying under a bush."

"No means—"

"No," the twins chorused.

"But she won't be a bother," Ricki pleaded.

"And if it is?"

"I'll set her free in the spring and she can be wild and die foaming at the mouth. Please, Liberty?"

"Who's going to feed it?"

"All of us."

"And who's going to clean up after it?"

"Isra will."

"I will not. Gross."

"We both will."

Liberty shook her head and put her hands on her hips.

Damn. It is cute, Liberty thought, glancing at Emma who was leaning against the wall behind Ricki. What do you have to do with this, Emma Nevada? Liberty asked with her eyes. Nothing, Emma signaled back, I am totally innocent this time. Liberty sighed. "Has it been fed yet?"

"She's not an it," Ricki said indignantly. "She's a she. I gave her some milk and Emma and me walked to the store for kitten food."

Nothing to do with this? Liberty shot in her look at Emma, who returned nothing. "Put that cat down and start picking up this house; it's a mess."

Liberty curved her hand down the cat's back, her fingers leaving small grooves in her fur. Tina Turner was a warm circle in Liberty's lap and she could feel her purring. Funny how I haven't stopped aching since the day Isra left, Liberty thought, laying her hand over her heart. Wish she'd stayed home. Wish I could sleep, I'll bet that's what it is. I'm just aching from that, so tired I feel like I've been running marathons instead of sleeping.

She looked out the window. The curtain sheers were a soft gray except where the lights from the other houses formed small golden halos around themselves. Looks colder than it is, always does in March. In like a lion, out like a lamb, whoever thought that up sure as hell didn't live here. She shook her head and glanced at the stereo. It was a new thing Ricki'd bought after their birthdays. Two tape decks, a turntable, all sorts of knobs and lights that she tried to show me. How do you work the radio? I asked. That's all I'm interested in. Good thing I found that out, Ricki's never home anymore, hit the road with the band to play in places I don't even want to think about her being in. But she's got to make her career, got to make a living, I guess. Well, with the radio and Tina Turner, I'm not alone, even though my children go off chasing their dreams.

*   *   *

This is a nightmare, Isra decided. That's the only way to describe this weather. I knew there was another reason why I left Minneapolis. Liberty looped her arm through Isra's, the only solidity against the invisible ice splinters blasting through her clothing and into her skin. On the interstate, Isra could see the other cars, their colors muted by the flying snow and dried slush on the taxi's window. Winter, I had to come back here in winter, she thought, struggling up the walk while leaning on her mother. What was I thinking, that the end of February was almost spring? And showing up alone. Caleb, you owe me for this.

"You want something to eat, maybe a cup of coffee?" Liberty asked, kicking off her snow boots and setting them on the radiator.

Isra kicked off her shoes. They're ruined, she decided, shoving them next to Liberty's boots. "I think I'll take a nap, sleep off the jet lag."

The house was exactly the same as she'd left it a little less than four months ago, except for a box marked Salvation Army in the middle of her old bedroom. Wonder what she's going to do with this room, Isra thought, climbing into her bed. She slept until the next evening, waking with a start. She dressed slowly, pulling on the lilac cashmere sweater Caleb had given her. Take it for the trip, he'd said, and pretend it's me wrapped around you.

"Sleep good?" Liberty asked as they sat in the living room.

"All right." Isra sipped her coffee. "This is good. Everybody in London drinks instant."

They sat for a moment, listening to the wind whip the snow around.

"How's Anderhazy's?"

"Fine. Why don't you come to work with me some time this week? Madame said she'd like to see you."

"Maybe. We'll see."

"You dancing much these days?"

"Not too much. My knee starts hurting like I don't know

what. Besides, between classes and auditions, I hardly have time."

As Liberty sipped her coffee, her heart seemed to hunch forward, crowding her lungs and making it difficult to breathe. She's not a dancer anymore, we're running out of dancers, Liberty thought, the steam from the coffee landing on her skin. Used to be all of us were a bunch of bodies dancing in a field. Now most of us have become pairs of eyes sitting in the dark, watching and watching.

"I've learned so much about my craft and Caleb's so supportive. He's a filmmaker and constantly helping me develop as an actress." Isra tapped her coffee cup with her fingernails, four clicks in a row, and set it on the end table next to the varnished box. "What are you going to do with this?"

"Keep it." Liberty set her cup down to pick up the box. This cat, even broken in half, is still the most beautiful thing I've ever seen, Emma, not including my girls.

Isra stood up and turned to the front windows. The snow had stuck to the screens. It's so white, so pure like that, she thought. As if it wants to be trusted. She dropped her head and turned to Liberty. "Caleb wanted to come with me on this trip, but he's in the middle of a project. We promised one another that our relationship wouldn't interfere with our work."

"Good luck with that part of it," Liberty said dryly.

Isra lifted her chin. "I hope you'll be happy for us."

Liberty got up out of the recliner and took the empty cups into the kitchen.

"You're not going to say anything?" Isra called at her back.

Liberty set the dishes in the sink. He's white. Otherwise she would've dragged him here. Her heart thudded as if getting shoved out of the way. Stop it, she thought, her hand flat against her chest. Suddenly, Liberty could feel a weight lying on her heart, dragging down every beat. Like a bullwhip tearing away at what I hold dear. Pushing her palm harder against her chest, she massaged slowly in a circle, feeling her bones solid against her skin. This has got to stop, she thought, walking back to the living room.

Isra was sitting on the couch again. "Don't you even want to meet him?"

"When I won't interfere with his work." Liberty shivered with the need to break down and free the sudden clawing pain scraping at the inside of her. There is a wild thing in me, she realized, gasping for a full breath, a wild thing wanting out. She sat back in her chair, concentrating on her breathing. Slow, she thought, rubbing her chest again. Take it easy.

"Are you all right, Liberty?"

"Fine, baby. Just got a pulled muscle. You know how it is." The pain eased with the warmth of her hand. Better. Better. "He's white, isn't he?"

"Yes."

Liberty's heart thudded again and for a moment she felt dizzy. Why did I ask that? Mamie is dead. Gone. This is a new time. What is this come to haunt me? she wondered, her mind feeling clouded.

"If you have some sort of prejudice—"

"No, baby." Liberty stopped her. "How could I have such a prejudice?"

"I don't care if Caleb's white, Liberty. He's taught me that race is unimportant; I don't even see his color anymore."

Isra watched as her mother slowly got out of her chair and walked out of the room. My god. I didn't think she was going to be so upset, she thought. What do I do now? She heard the bedroom door close. Is she angry with me? Isra walked quietly down the hall to her old room. Inside, she leaned against the wall. It was cold against her face as she strained to hear. Just the radio, WCCO, probably. She stepped out and edged to Liberty's closed door. Nothing but the radio. Carefully, sure to miss the squeaky board in front of the linen closet in the hall, she returned to the living room. What did I do for Liberty to be angry about? Because he's white? Is that it? It couldn't be. Damn it. Caleb, love, I wish you were here. Is she mad about that? He would've come, but I told him not to, he's busy right now and I didn't want to wait to tell Liberty. Is that it?

"What should I do, Tina Turner?" she asked the cat curled up in Liberty's chair.

Liberty sighed again, massaging the aching place between her breasts, then ran a hand down the cat's neck, admiring the smooth gray fur. Even Tina Turner is getting old, there's silver on her muzzle. "I don't like cats, do you know that, Tina Turner?" she whispered, not wanting to wake her daughter.

The cat looked up at Liberty.

"But I like you. Emma said I would." She chuckled. "Just you wait, Tina Turner. Someday an army of gray-haired old women are going to take over the world. And leading the pack will be me with my transistor radio."

The sky grew lighter. I must be getting old, sitting here wanting to cry over my kids taking their own way. I knew it was going to happen, hell, I trained them for it, but I can't believe it. Not that I want to be twenty-one again, hear. At least I got the sound of the radio keeping ghosts in hiding. That is a fact. Mamie, Cherise, Terry, Emma. Radio gives me old music and new music and keeps all my ghosts standing back. But those lonesome blues—Israellen will be singing the lonesome blues about this Caleb. She says she doesn't even see his color; what that means is he's denying hers. Worst of all, she's busy dismissing her own race to be with him, giving up her inheritance, erase who she is. Trying to believe it's unimportant. Huh. Why doesn't he go to Hollywood and leave my girl alone?

Later that morning, after Liberty had gone to work, Madame, her voice creakier than ever, called. A student had found Liberty in number three dance studio; the ambulance had taken her to St. Mary's-Riverside Hospital on Franklin Avenue. Isra rushed to get dressed. When she arrived, Madame Anderhazy was sitting on a couch, nodding the way old people do. She said nothing, only patted the young woman's hand before leaving the hospital. Isra paced the corridor after the doctor left, keeping her arms tight against her, afraid to touch anything.

At the beginning of the hour a nurse led her to Liberty's small dark room. A massive coronary, a doctor told her. Isra looked at her mother's face. I never noticed the lines before, she thought, never noticed the thin strands of silver in her hair. She's old. Isra squeezed her eyes shut then opened them slowly. But she is Liberty, still. She will always be Liberty Grace Jones; luck, love or her daughters have never changed that. For one brief shining moment, Israellen wished she had her mother's face and all Liberty's years of living behind her. All the things she's seen and known, all the strength she carries. Isra leaned over the bed, fists clenched and her back tight, willing Liberty to live. She could've sworn the room was brighter as if Liberty's soul paused, wavering between her still, weak body and wherever souls go when they've finally given up.

"Time's up," the nurse called softly from the door.

Isra crossed her arms again as she walked back to the waiting room. The nurse had said Liberty needed rest. Isra realized that meant she would sleep until her body decides to live or die. Isra curled up in a chair, eyes burning, trying to sleep between the five-minute visits. During the last, a thin sliver of spit had fallen from Liberty's mouth, and Isra had wiped it away with the corner of the bedsheet. Liberty—the thought trailed away like smoke. There was nothing now, not even the relief of imagination. Just time. Isra threw off the small hospital blanket she'd found at the end of a couch and stood up, a hard ache in her lower back. She paced again.

Glancing out the window, she noticed gray puddles of melted snow. Spring is trying to show up. A small tree was beginning to bud, she'd seen their hard jackets shining with the light of the morning sun when she'd gotten out of the cab and run into the hospital. It must hurt when the leaves burst from the trees, why else would spring hesitate? From the fifth floor she could see the tree, reaching up to the warmth and arching with the wind. I was once that limber, once as able to bend. She stretched her arms over her head trying to work the kink out of her back. Once I was the prima donna. She smiled, her lips together.

Pressing her palm against the glass, she could feel the rush of the wind shaking the window.

Wind for kites. A big wind needs a big kite, Emma Nevada would say. How old were we, three? She came home with the biggest, brightest kite I've ever seen and it practically took off with me and Ricki hanging onto the end. But that's not all she brought, Isra realized, looking at the small tree again before turning away. Ricki knew it automatically. Ricki knew like she'd gone along, traveling in Emma's back pocket.

"White people are so surprised we're angry." Emma sipped her coffee, the purple rings around her eyes betraying her tiredness. "But people are always surprised by everything, snow in winter, sun in the summer. Hey, look at that little one over there, she's just about to slide right out of her seat, she's so sleepy."

You're getting pretty big for this, little girls, Liberty thought as she carried Isra to her bedroom, Emma following with Rickshaw slung over her back like a sack of potatoes.

"Look at this kid," Emma chuckled, pointing to Ricki's little butt. "I'll bet she could sleep through a hurricane."

They tucked the twins in, each getting a kiss right between the eyebrows, and walked back to the kitchen. Liberty examined her best friend. She was thinner than ever; it wasn't healthy for her to be as close to her bones as that.

"Ever notice how some people spend their lives trying to keep their noses above trouble while other people just walk right over it like Jesus on the water?"

"You mean white people?"

"Hell, I don't know what I mean. My ability to think seems to be slipping right out of my fingers these days." Emma shook her head again and slouched in the chair. "Do you remember the night Blind Harold Washington played for us after Travis told him he didn't need any more horns? That Travis. Some men aren't worth the time it takes to forget a bad idea. But do you remember? All those people piled into the crummy tent and Blind Harold pulls out that sax and starts blowing, I could just see walls falling from people's eyes. That fat old man with his beat-up saxophone was lacing up so many pieces of misery and knotting them up like string. Made an echo in me that hasn't stopped yet. When was that?"

"Nineteen fifty-two."

Emma coughed suddenly. "I quit smoking. Think I have lung cancer now."

Liberty stood up and reached for a bottle from the cupboard above the refrigerator. "Then you ought to have some medicine," she said, opening the whiskey and dumping a shot into each cup.

Emma took a slug of her coffee. "I feel better already. It's a miracle of holiness, as my grandmother would say."

She gestured with her cup and Liberty poured more whiskey. Emma nodded to herself and leaned forward to rest her chin in her hand. "Jealousy. Jealousy is poison."

"Jealousy?" Liberty asked, then sipped from her cup. "What in the hell are you talking about?"

"Black people wanting what white people got."

"Jealousy means wanting something that you never will have and didn't really want in the first place."

"You sound like Cherise."

"Cherise was right. What do white people got that any self-respecting Negro doesn't?"

"Self-respect."

"Think white people going to give you that? I got self-respect, with or without their permission."

"Then you're one of two niggers in America who does."

"You got self-respect."

Emma pointed a finger at herself. "One." She swung her finger at Liberty. "And two."

Their laughter, soft as it was, faded under the hum of the refrigerator.

"Emma? How you fixed for money?"

"I get along. What I can't get from the Movement, I pick up

playing music. I've gotten pretty good on that guitar. It's all I need right now."

"You on the stage again?"

"Only if you consider living rooms and college dormitories the stage. I don't know how much longer I can keep performing. I've heard too many white children trying to play like Leadbelly or Ivory Joe, trying to sing like Miss Bessie. Makes my fists tie up in knots. Can't play with knotted fingers and twisted guts like that, you know."

Isra flattened her slim hand against the window glass again. My hands are naturally graceful, she thought absently, like Madame said. How many times me and Ricki would hold hands as we walked down the street or balanced on the railroad tracks, looking more like a picture of racial harmony than sisters? Until we were six or seven, we held hands everywhere we went, like we were each other's best defense. Then I started dancing every day, and she'd given up on ever learning— Liberty once said she thought I'd gotten all the grace and balance we both were to have. We all realized Ricki's inability to remember right from left also accounted for her always being late, her horrible handwriting and not being able to read. Dyslexia. I learned the word too late, long after the damage was done. Why don't you read that to me, I'd say to her, pointing at a book or a sign. Why don't you tell me what it says? And Ricki'd just stare at me like I was trying to break her up in little pieces.

Ricki, where the hell are you? Liberty is dying. She is dying and there is no one but me to help her. Get your passing white ass up here, I can't do this alone.

What if Ricki doesn't want to see me? She didn't make plans to see me even when she knew I'd be visiting. Seems like she left on purpose. On the road, Liberty said. On the road from February to the end of March, left two days before I arrived. Isra breathed deeply, the medicated air of the hospital filling

151

her lungs. She can't think I—but I had nothing to do with Angel leaving. I had nothing to do with Angel at all. She just showed up, dragging that painting she said she had to finish. I had nothing to do with it, Ricki. I only met her once.

Isra studied the woman sitting in Liberty's chair. She's very good looking, better looking than that washed-out Nadine, she decided. "How long were you in England?"

"Few months," Angel answered. "Got some friends living on the southeast end of London, I'm sure you could stay with them. Sort of run-down, but cheap."

"I'm not worried about money," Isra said quickly.

"They are." Angel grinned. "At least you'd have people to show you around."

"That would be great."

A car horn honked.

Ricki finished rolling up her sleeves and glanced out the front windows. "That's the guys. Isra, you riding with us or not?"

"I'll wait for Liberty."

"Liberty knows how to get to Johnny's bar."

"I could give you a ride," Angel suggested. "Nicer than taking the bus."

Isra considered it. "Okay."

"Wonderful," Ricki said, grabbing her guitar. "See you in about an hour, okay?"

Liberty and Isra followed Angel to a small table between the bar and the stage. The place wasn't packed, Isra noticed, but there were more people than the last time. And at least they're not all drunk and slumped over the bar, she thought, setting down her purse and crossing her legs.

"I've never been in such a little car before in my life," Liberty said.

"It's a Fiat, Liberty. A sports car."

"It's still too small. Gives me claustrophobia."

Angel waved a waitress over. "What are you drinking?"

"Gin and tonic," Isra replied, the first thing she could think of.

"Ginger ale," Liberty said. "Doesn't look like they're starting yet. I'm going to put a quarter in the jukebox."

Angel and Isra watched her go.

"I like her," Angel said simply, pulling out a cigarette.

"Hold that opinion till you hear which songs she picks, always the kind old people sing along with. May I have a cigarette?"

"Help yourself."

Nothing good, Liberty decided. No "Bye, Bye Blackbird," nothing by Brook Benton and what kind of jukebox would leave out the songs of Brook Benton? Not one getting my quarters, that's for sure. She checked out the rest of the bar. Different crowd than usual for this place, my girl must be getting herself some fans. Liberty glanced at their table. That Angel, seems nice enough but there's something about her makes me think she'll never be satisfied till she can grow wings and fly over the rest of us. Guess her name fits her just right. But Ricki's fallen for someone she can't have and that's not right at all. She must've gotten her way of falling in love from her daddy. Seems she got all sorts of things from her daddy but himself. Angel held a cigarette lighter so Isra, her hand on the girl's wrist, could light a cigarette. Isra smoking. That is a nasty, filthy habit.

"Thank you," Isra said as Angel set the lighter back on the table.

"So am I supposed to call your mother Mrs. Jones or Liberty or what?"

"She's not missus. She's never been a missus and even if she was she'd probably smack your face for calling her so. Call her Liberty and see if she objects."

Liberty watched the stage. There's Yaz, looking as corrupt and bent over as ever. He's got to be sixty if not older. And Marcel on the drums. Reminds me of those old days, Terry Cee's dance band jamming in the basement, days and nights filled with people making music. She shook her head and searched for Ricki. Somebody was on the floor messing with a pile of wires, that must be her. She looked closer. Yep. My daughter, on her knees in those new fifty-dollar jeans.

Ricki set down the effects board. That'll do it. Trust Marcel to slice clean through the cables, hacked right through them by dropping that cymbal. Took a chunk out of that, too. Who gives a damn? We'll fix all this shit, get ourselves a trailer to haul it in, and start touring. Get out and play for my people, watch them grooving to my music. She got to her feet and glanced across the room. Not here yet. No, there they are. Over by the bar.

Liberty sat down in her chair and smiled at her daughter. She's looking good, my Ricki is.

Ricki smiled back. We got to rock tonight, she thought.

"You got that fixed, baby?" Yaz said, clapping a hand on her shoulder. He was wearing the shades she'd given him and looking sharp.

"I think so. Give it a run?"

Yaz nodded his head. Ricki picked up her Stratocaster and slung the strap over her shoulder, loosening it to hang just a little lower against her hips. Okay, beauty, she thought, looking at the guitar. We're going to color this whole room blue.

Isra set her empty glass down. "When are they supposed to start?"

Ricki stepped on the amp's stand-by button and a hum filled the room. We got it, she thought, grinning suddenly in anticipation at Yaz. He didn't grin back, but instead blew a single clean blue-filled note into the room.

Israellen got drunk, then drunker, and finally so drunk somebody had to carry her out to the tiny little car. She remembered Angel's angular face and a smile like sunshine on glass when she woke up the next morning. Ricki walked into her bedroom carrying a bottle of aspirin and a glass of pineapple juice.

"Shut up and drink it. What did you think of Angel?"

Isra moaned. Her mouth felt furry, she stank of cigarette smoke, and her head felt like someone had peeled back her scalp to let in a thousand little red devils to pound on her skull with nasty little ice picks. Gin and tonics, she thought. Cigarettes. "What time is it?"

"Two in the afternoon. Drink this, it'll help. Wish you'd learn to handle your liquor." She dropped the aspirin bottle on Isra's stomach. "Take a few of these, too. Well?"

"Well what?"

"What did you think?"

"She's very nice. Now go away and let me die."

Ricki chuckled and walked out. Isra gulped down some aspirin and juice, then lay there watching the ceiling spin. She squeezed her eyes shut, but no good; the whole room got into the act, her closet, her desk, her bed, even her clothes all started playing merry-go-round with her in the middle.

"Hey, Isra, you want to—" Ricki walked back in. "Oh, shit!" She grabbed Isra's arms and dragged her out of bed to the bathroom.

"Oh, god, oh god," she mumbled over and over, her voice echoing back. The cat wandered in, stood on her back legs to peer at the toilet bowl and how far Isra's head was in it.

"Well, what do you say to this, Tina Turner? Look at her," Ricki pointed. "She's turned the color of vanilla ice cream."

Tina Turner sat in the middle of the rug, looking up at Ricki.

"Drank like a goddamn fish," Ricki went on, "And after Liberty left, she tried to pick up some slimy guy, then one tried to pick up her, then she disappeared with both of them for about half an hour. I thought I was a fast operator."

"I did not," Isra said feebly.

"Then some other guy offered her some coke and if I hadn't stopped her, she'd have flown home under her own power."

Isra staggered to her feet and leaned over the sink. She splashed some water onto her face and into her mouth, then looked in the mirror. "I didn't do any of those things," she said to her twin's reflection. "Did I?"

Ricki had picked up the cat and started humming "What More Can a Woman Do." She broke off and let the cat jump out of her arms. "What'd you think of the band?"

"I remember thinking you were pretty good, but I'm not sure."

"Girl, you are a mess. Get some sleep." Ricki got halfway down the hall. "Oh, yeah. The airline called. Said your reservation is confirmed."

"Thanks," Isra said weakly.

We rocked last night like that bar was a cradle and all of them were unruly children. Ricki's whole body shook like the groove had aftershocks. She picked up the phone and dialed Angel's number. No answer. She must be working, Ricki thought. She always unplugs the phone when she's working.

But there was no answer for three days. Then Angel called.

Ricki sat on the bus into downtown watching the old women. She liked old women. She liked the soft parts of their arms and the way they smelled. She liked the delicate sturdiness of their faces and the way their mouths set when they crossed the street. She remembered the time an old woman was hit by a car as she crossed Lake Street. Ricki could feel the indignity still. The woman's skirt was pulled to the top of her stockings and her wig had come off and her hair lay curled around her head in a mess of bobby pins. Ricki had wanted to shout stop staring, she's not a circus animal. Traffic should halt when an old woman wants to cross. An old woman should wear silk and linen and should have someone else to clean her house.

Ricki watched her lover cross the loft toward her. "Why did you call me, Angel?"

Liquor sloshed over the edge of the glass Angel was holding as she leaned over to plant a sharp kiss on Ricki's mouth. "Did I call you? You haven't just been here all the time, large as life and twice as natural?"

Ricki looked away from her to the city below. Moonlight fell on the roofs wet with rain and shattered into a million pieces, and under one traffic light was a pool of rubies. Why do you do this? Ricki thought suddenly. Why do you make it so bad when it could be so good? She turned slowly as Angel leaned towards her, close enough so Ricki could feel her breath on her face.

Angel reached up one hand and cupped Ricki's chin. "You have the strangest eyes I've ever seen, so green, like sea water when the sun strikes it. If eyes are the window to the soul, you sure as hell have one."

"Emma Nevada used to say a soul was a goddamn nuisance. Can't dump it, can't even sell it to the devil he's got so much business for free these days." She turned away to look at the painting on the easel.

"I think I'm going to call this one 'A Contemporary Alice.' What do you think?"

Ricki rubbed her eyes. Up late jamming and talking about upcoming gigs with Yaz and Mal, she was feeling a little out-of-focus. She could smell cigarettes and the wood polish she used for the Strat on her hands mixing with linseed oil and that strange scent she found only with Angel. Ricki looked at the painting again. It's definitely someone. Who? Only the hands are near to finished. Staring, suddenly her breath caught somewhere between her heart and her mouth as a rush of adrenaline tightened the muscles in her legs. Hands act, speak, tell things, and Ricki's clenched fists were a giveaway to her nervousness and hope. Is it me? Those look like my hands. She clasped hers behind her back where they comforted one another like frightened children. It must be, Ricki thought. Her throat hurt to ask. It must be me.

Isra could see her reflection in the waiting room television screen. Her forehead was stretched, her eyes wide and no chin. I had nothing to do with Angel's leaving. She'd given me the address to this flat and suddenly there she was. Just Angel— she does what she wants. She showed me that painting, said she had come all this way so she could finish it. A week, a month, I fell in love with Caleb and time sped right past me. She still hadn't finished when I left London.

"You have a perfect body."

Isra toweled off her face. A single drop of sweat trailed down her neck and Angel wiped it away.

"You won't be much of an actor if you can't control your face, Isra." Once Angel had said it was strange how Isra would push her body to the limit but wouldn't take the touch of another woman.

Isra looked away. "When do you leave for Florence?"

"Does it matter?"

She hung the towel on the back of a chair and pulled on a cotton robe over her leotard. "You committed yourself."

Angel watched as the light fabric flew around Isra's body, then tightened in a swift neat knot at her waist. "I'll get there when I get there."

Isra looped the towel around her neck like a prize fighter. "Someday, Angel, someday, you aren't going to get what you ask for."

"When I have to ask, darling, I'll get into a different line of work." She glanced beyond the dusty windowsill to the city below.

Isra looked, too, letting London fill her vision. So different from Minneapolis, she thought. She shook her head, as if the pictures she remembered were an Etch-A-Sketch that could be erased. "Get enough drawings?"

Angel shook her head. "They're not right," she answered, bouncing her toe on the wooden floor. "But I have an idea."

Isra followed Angel into the Underground, getting out at Marble Arch and walking through the pedestrian subway into Hyde Park. It was chilly, but the winter rain had stopped, and large puddles gathered in the road because the gutters were blocked. It's still dirty, Isra noticed, this city is still a mess after the rain. A bus rolled by, a huge sheet of water rising up from the tires like a fan and hit the sidewalk like a split-second of thundering applause. Isra liked this park. She liked the quiet and the swans with their feet that looked like maple leaves in autumn. As the clouds broke and the sun shone a spectacular sunset, Angel leaned against the dry side of a huge oak tree.

"Beautiful," she said, looking at the clouds, cherry red with tinges of purple. "Like you."

Isra glanced at her feet. How many more times will she say that before my stomach won't do a back flip?

"Aren't you going to agree?"

"I agree." She glanced up. "The sky is beautiful."

"Most women get a little flustered when I say things like that."

"Don't you think the sky looks like a painting?"

"But you don't," Angel continued.

"You're a painter, you should know." Isra stared at her.

Angel pushed away from the oak tree and down the path, Isra beside her. "You're used to it, aren't you?"

"To what?"

"Being told that you are beautiful."

"Aren't you? Someone must've told you that you're beautiful."

"My mother. When I was a tiny little girl."

"How about your lovers?"

"Someone who wants to fuck you will tell you anything." Angel kicked a small stone down the path.

"Is that why you tell me I'm beautiful?"

"I'm an artist."

"I'm an actor. Does it make a difference?"

Angel stopped again. "No."

"Caleb says my looks are my ticket in."

"What does he know?"

"He knows films."

"He knows gossip."

"He's serious."

"They're all serious till they have to work."

"What makes you any different?"

"Nothing." Angel's face was neutral.

They didn't speak on the subway ride back to Isra's flat. Isra sat down on a pillow in the small living room, leaning against the wall. "How much longer will it take you to finish the painting?"

"However long it takes."

"I leave for Minneapolis in three days."

"When will you be back?"

"The beginning of March."

"We'll start over then."

"Start over? What's the matter with what you have?"

"I'm going to change the painting." Angel set down her cup and ran her finger around the edge. "To a nude."

"What makes you think I'd pose for you?"

"Because I want you to."

Their eyes met and tangled. In her look, Isra could feel Angel reaching for her, touching her. Don't do this, she thought, breaking away to look out the window. The sky was deep gray, no longer a painting, and the sun a dull silver coming through the wide glass. She sipped her coffee and watched Angel light a cigarette. From here, Isra decided, her eyes are blacker than black.

Isra stepped away from the television and went back to the hospital window. She pushed her hand to the glass again, her palm feeling colder than the rest of her. Outside, the young tree was still reaching for the sky. Pulling her hand away, she slowly curled her fingers into a fist and let them relax outward again. Like a magic trick, she thought absently.

She paced the floor. Reaching the corner, she turned to follow the aluminum strip that separated the orange-and-brown carpet from linoleum. She stuck out her arms to balance on the metal like a tightrope walker.

"Aren't you going to try?" Isra asked, balancing on the railroad track, showing off.

"Don't want to," Ricki answered, dropping her jacket and tugging at the spike halfway out of the railroad tie. Wish you'd quit that and start working, she thought, hoping Isra would read her mind. We came down here to get these, why don't you do some work?

They were going to gather as many spikes as they could and soak them in a bucket half water and half Bon Ami cleanser. After dinner, they would scrub them with old toothbrushes till the rust and crud fell off like peeling skin. Underneath, they were sure, were new, shiny black railroad spikes, and if they scrubbed long enough, ignoring the way their skin would pucker and sting from the water, they would have those brand new things for their very own. Isra said she'd keep hers in a secret place forever; Ricki thought she'd sell hers back to the railroad and buy a real amplifier to replace the Silvertone Liberty had bought at a garage sale for two dollars.

"Ricki?"

"Yeah?"

"Want to go to the library? Mrs. Tjarden said you could find out anything in the library."

"I heard her." Ricki kicked the spike and put her hands on her hips. "You going to help?"

Isra tightroped down the track. "Bet there's a book about ballerinas. Don't you like ballerinas?"

"No."

"I bet there's a book about anything you want to know about. Mrs. Tjarden said so."

"Not everything the teacher says is true, Israellen."

"Bet she's right about the library."

"Fine!" Ricki shouted suddenly, grabbing her jacket, the two spikes she'd already found flying into the air.

"Wait!" Isra shouted, digging them out of the weeds and racing after her.

Ricki asked the librarian about God and the woman showed her a row of kids' Bible books.

She just stared at the woman. "I don't want no book, lady, I want you to tell me."

Isra elbowed her in the side.

"Stop it, Isra," Ricki ordered.

The librarian thought for a second then led us into the audio room. There were shelves of records, one on just about everything, she said. Stories, music, anything. She showed Ricki where the record player was and made us promise not to break anything. Two seconds later Mahalia Jackson was singing through the little earphones we had to wear. And Ricki figured a way to get through school from first grade on by listening and listening, taking it all in.

Isra glanced at the waiting-room pay phone. I've called Caleb once and he'll be here as soon as he can. I wish I could hear him, just hear him talking.

His voice was as silken as the lapels on the jacket he'd been wearing. Do you like it? he'd asked her. Her answer was to take it and the rest of his clothes off. Angel hates him, Isra thought, looking out her bedroom window. The moon scattered its sequins on the road and hung silver beads on the trees and the railing on the small balcony. I didn't even realize it rained again. Now it's so quiet and looks lovely. She glanced at Caleb sleeping quietly next to her. How gentle he is, she thought. Very sweet. She glanced out the window again. Isra felt a heaviness in her chest, like she'd swallowed a fist; maybe it's my soul rising up to meet the moon.

She slipped out of bed as quietly as she could to not disturb him. Tying on her robe, Isra walked into the bare living room. The half-empty bottle of wine and the glasses sat in the middle of the floor. She sat down on a pillow, taking a glass. Angel's sketch was hanging on the opposite wall, a charcoal sketch of Isra dancing. The drawing was the only gift she had ever accepted from Angel.

"Just take the goddamn thing," she'd said, tearing it out of her sketchpad and shoving it into Isra's hands, then walking out the door.

*   *   *

The note was scrawled on a piece of drawing paper torn out of Angel's sketchpad, Ricki realized, running her finger along the jagged edge. She tried the door to Angel's loft once again. She gritted her teeth and began tracing the letters on the note with her finger. Slowly, the words came to her: Goodbye. It was fun. I've gone to London.

London. Damn you, Angel. Folding up the note, she jammed it in her pocket. Ricki knew for a certainty. London. Israellen. Isra. Damn you, baby sister. She hurried out of the freight elevator to the bus stop, her pace quickening with each step. A block away, Ricki burst into a full run, the hard pounding of her feet on the concrete rippling through her body.

Boff called at two. Papa May called at six, both of them wanting to know where Ricki was. At nine, Yaz called.

"Where is she, Liberty Grace? We're supposed to be bopping right now."

"I don't know, Hezekiah."

"What happened?"

"Your guess is as good as mine. She walked right past me and out the door before I could say two words."

"Okay," he said, his hoarse voice gentle. "I'll find her."

Ricki was at the Dew Drop Inn, hunched over a beer.

"What's going on, baby?" Yaz asked, climbing onto the stool next to her.

"Nothing, man."

He glanced around the bar. "You shouldn't be hanging at a place like this, baby. Cops'll get you for misusing your color."

She didn't say anything, just kept staring at the light above the bar.

"Damn, girl, I know you're in bad shape when you don't fly back on a comment like that."

Ricki sipped her beer and carefully set the glass back on the cardboard coaster.

"I talked to your mama tonight. That friend of yours, the one with all the hair, who is that?"

"Papa May."

"Why you would want to do that to your own head I will never know. Ain't you afraid of getting it caught on fire or trapped in an elevator door with it all knotted up like that? Anyhow, he called to find out where you were. Said you didn't show up to jam."

"Had other things on my mind."

"Other than music?" He whistled a low note. "You shouldn't lie like that."

The bartender sauntered over and stood in front of Yaz. "You want anything?"

"Bring my wife another and I'll have the same. And a shot of Windsor, too."

The bartender glanced at Ricki then back at him, rolling her eyes as she walked away.

"You ought to call your mama, she's worried about you."

Liberty should know better than that, Ricki thought, finishing her beer just as the bartender set the next round in front of them.

"Thanks, sugar. Pay the lady, Ricki."

Ricki pulled out her wallet, her extreme care showing how drunk she was. The bartender scooped up the money and walked away, leaving them to sit hip to hip and lean against the bar just as hundreds of other people had, watching foam slide down the sides of a glass.

"She's gone."

"Who?" Yaz slurped down some whiskey.

"Angel."

"Well." He slapped back the rest of his shot and chased it with beer.

She glanced into her wallet in the secret place behind the dollar bills, behind the newspaper clipping about Bessie Smith's gravestone. There, folded like a Japanese fan. Goodbye. It was fun. I've gone to London. Gone to get my baby sister, Ricki thought, jamming her wallet into her pocket. Meet up with Isra, going to fuck her brains out, Angel? Who next? Liberty? Ricki sipped her beer, trying to push away the hot, brassy taste of anger. "So now what am I supposed to do?"

"That stuff happens."

"Don't break your neck trying to be sympathetic."

"You don't need sympathy, girl."

"No?"

"No. I'm not saying she did you a favor by breaking your heart, but that's how it is and that's some place for you to start."

"Start what? The only thing I'm thinking of starting is another bottle," she muttered, drinking her beer.

"Some people like desire more than they like pleasure. Some jazz musicians, not the great ones, mind, but some good ones, would rather want than get. They like new for the sake of new and misery for its messiness. Now I can understand that—if you don't know how to get, then wanting is the next best thing." Yaz pulled out his Lucky Strikes. "How long we known each other? Let's see, you were sixteen, seventeen, maybe. Asking me to jam with you, play on some album. Shit, I thought, here comes this gal wanting to play the blues. Five, six years, now, and I have to say that you're finally on your way, Ricki. This is the blues. This is the real news. You *got* love. Now you lost love and you're stuck with it, baby."

"I never wanted this, never."

"You want love and you want to sing the blues. Damn hard to get them both. Most times the two is mutually exclusive." His voice swung low on the last two words, hitting every syllable. "And so we have a drink. We have a smoke. We have another drink and a few laughs of the wrong kind. Then we play."

"Just like that?"

"Just like that. Then we'll see how far we get."

I wonder how far Ricki is, Isra thought, pacing another length of the floor. She must have gotten my message. I hope she got the message. I don't know how much longer I can sit alone in this goddamn hospital, waiting for a miracle or a disaster. She dragged her fingers softly over her face. Hands make the air ready to receive you. How cold Liberty's hands were, the veins stuck out along the backs, her nails like ivory against her skin and her skin darker against the white sheets of the bed.

Out, I want to go outside, just for a minute, Isra thought. I need fresh air. If I have to walk back and forth here any longer I will go insane. Forty-five minutes before the top of the hour. She grabbed her jacket, pulling it on violently as she rushed for the elevator.

Ricki sat on a Greyhound bus, wishing she could fold herself up like one of the shirts in her duffel bag and sit indifferent. Instead, she was framed in the tinted window, watching Texas go by—Giddings, Lexington, Cameron, Rosebud, Lott— on the way to Waco. Rubbing her eyes, she wished for sleep or at least her Walkman and some tapes. Used to carry my cassettes always. Music. A talking book. I remember I stole *Alice in Wonderland* and *Through the Looking Glass* right after I met Angel so I could get her jokes. She never asked about those books again and I never had the chance to show off my new knowledge.

I hope Liberty doesn't die. Please get me to the airport, please let me get there on time. Seems like I'm always late, just a beat behind when somebody needs me. Always. Isra, Liberty, Angel, Yaz. Poor Hezekiah, always seem to miss him when he's in need. Should've taken his advice and brought a bottle. Cuts down the time, cuts back everything but the sound of the tires on the road.

Yaz was rocking as he leaned against the wall of a building on Nicollet Mall. Just rocking back and forth, a little crooked but on the beat all the same. As soon as she saw him, Ricki'd pushed through a crush of commuters who made stupid sounds as she stepped on their feet or smacked them with her guitar. It was two blocks before she got off the packed bus and hurried back to find him.

"Yaz." She reached for his arm.

His eyes were squeezed shut and he was humming a little scrap of a song.

"Hezekiah, it's me."

He slowly opened one eye. He was so drunk, the white was yellow and lined with red veins. "Ricki."

She nodded, listening to the melody he was humming over and over, one of his songs called, "Here Come the Honeyman."

Opening his other eye, Yaz gripped the hand resting on his arm. "Hey, babe, what's going on? You want a drink?" He pointed at the bottle standing next to his open saxophone case.

"No, man, thanks. What you doing down here?"

"Making a little coin, sugar. Hey, you got your guitar, let's jam. Just a little, okay?" He picked up Miss Julie, his horn. "Take out your fiddle."

Ricki glanced around for cops, then set her guitar case on the ground. Good as any place, she thought, and we're late for band practice anyway.

He ran off few licks.

"Sounding good, man," she said. She pulled out her portable amp, switched to battery power and clamped it to her belt loop. She ducked her arm and head through the guitar strap. "You ready?"

Pulling his shades over his eyes, he blew a single wailing note then dropped three more as if tears could come out of the bell of a saxophone. It was the song he'd been humming, a deep blues. She strummed out a minor to match the ache in the music and slowly added the rhythm section to paint the background. Feel for it, Yaz had told her, you got to feel the blues, you don't count it out, you don't listen for it. You got to feel the beat coming to you. Ricki closed her eyes and opened her skin, let the sounds fall on her like rain does other people. There on the street, him in a stained raincoat with a new streak of dirt down the front, and her in a jean jacket, swaying to the sounds,

167

the two of them played the blues and didn't notice the sun throwing long shadows over the now-empty mall.

"Yaz," she said, taking off her guitar. "Man, we got to get out of here."

"One more, babe." He stuck the mouthpiece into his mouth.

"No, Yaz, they been waiting for us at rehearsal and I don't even think I can play anymore."

Slowly, Yaz unhooked the sax from its strap and placed each piece of Miss Julie back into her case. He patted her once before throwing a cloth over the shining silver and locked the case. "Nicest lady I've ever known."

"She's beautiful, Yaz," Ricki said, her gear already packed and now leading him to the bus shelter. "What were you doing down here, man?"

"Playing music. Drinking wine. You know my bad teeth?" he said, pointing at his jaw.

"Yeah."

"I saw a dentist, Said they're going to have to come out."

"Yeah? So? We'll find the money—"

"It ain't the money, Rickshaw. I'm losing my teeth."

"Shit, motherfucker, you are vain. You're ugly, got crooked eyes and you limp, now you're worried about that? Hell, man, you'll be dead and wondering what kind of suit to wear at the funeral." She shook her head as an 18 bus stopped. "Not that one, man, the next one."

"I'm losing my teeth. I'll lose my embouchure."

"Your what?"

"Embouchure. You know. What makes my mouth fit the horn."

It struck her then. "This dentist sure?"

"Yeah," he shook his head. "And the dentist is a she. What is the world coming to?"

What is the world coming to? I get a call from my baby sister because Liberty Grace is in the hospital. I always thought Liberty was indestructible, could count on her like the wind.

Yaz and the rest of the band left in Greenvine, Texas. Be back soon as I can, I said to them. Don't cancel all the dates. Damn. Who cares about music when Liberty's dying? She ain't dying. People have heart attacks and live all the time. Ricki looked out the window. The flatlands sped past, the picture slipping from the window frame and away, lost in the vast gray-green land outside the tinted bus window. Wish I could push these things I'm thinking right through the glass, leaving them there on the side of the freeway like signposts. Wonder how many other thoughts like mine clutter up the countryside? Wonder how long I'll have to think things like this?

"Five minutes," the nurse said. Israellen followed her to Liberty's room. Only five minutes. People dying and their children only get five minutes to see them. Isra gripped Liberty's hand, now a collection of thin sticks. For a moment, a picture swept over Isra, flooding her eyes: a huge dark ocean was pulling Liberty away and only the grip of her daughter's hand would keep her onshore. I can't let go, Liberty, Isra thought suddenly, the tears on her lashes splintering the light into thousands of rainbows. I can't let go of you yet. She took a deep breath and leaned over the bed.

"Ricki will be here soon," she said softly. "I found her in Texas."

Standing up straight, Isra took a deep breath. When the body fails, hearing holds out till the last possible minute, so maybe someone dying can get the last scrap of news that may bring them right back to life. Please, God, I hope she heard what I said, maybe she'll hang on till Ricki gets here. After listening to all the trouble my big sister has surely gotten into, no way will Liberty even think of checking out.

Covering her mother's hand in both of hers, Isra squeezed the cold fingers gently, massaging them in her palm. It was a trick Caleb taught her. He would rub her hands gently like this when she got a headache. First her hands, then her wrists, he would manipulate the muscles into loosening. She wanted him. Suddenly. She wanted him like she had at first, wanted him all over her all at the same time. She wanted him inside her and she wanted to be inside him. Surrounded. Isra wanted them to be surrounded by one another, mixed up in each other's skin till they blended like water into water.

"Time's up," another nurse said.

Isra focused on her mother again. Hang on, Liberty. Gently, Isra lay her hand back on the white sheet, her nerve endings quivering from the sudden hunger for him that calmed with each step back to the waiting room.

She paced again, counting the orange-and-brown diamonds patterning the waiting room carpet, arching her back to ease the tightness. She was starting to get a devil bite between her shoulder blades. Get one if you don't warm up, Liberty would explain. Get one if you're out of shape or you've been in the same position too long and the only thing that helps is a hot bath. I remember Emma once stuck in that when Ricki and I grew up, we'd be getting devil bites in all sorts of unexpected places that would need all sorts of remedies.

Walking back and forth won't bring the dead back to life, but she kept on. I'll be damned if I'm going to park my ass for another minute. A surge of rebellion rushed through her. No way, no more of this bullshit, somebody's got to tell me what's going on. She glanced at the nurses' station, a white smooth-topped desk between her and the Intensive Care rooms. They've got to know something by now. I'm the only one Liberty can count on. Ricki's somewhere between here and Waco, watching time till she arrives. I never knew that time isn't ticked off by a clock but in the miles between places. I'm twenty steps to Liberty and I can't move till the top of the hour.

Isra swung around, pacing the floor. Sometimes you got to let off a few fireworks, that's what Emma Nevada used to say, let people know you're more than just polite. I'm going to march over there and make them tell me what's really happening.

*   *   *

"Right on!"

"That's not it, Israellen," said her twin. "You got to look meaner. Like this."

Ricki slit her eyes and cocked her head. "Right on!" She punched her fist in the air. "Mr. Charlie going to be jammed up tight, beat down to his socks when the brothers and the sisters get tired of laying dead, they going to get funky and dance on his face, dig me?"

"That's pretty good," Isra said admiringly.

"I heard it on the radio."

"What's it mean?"

"What do you mean what's it mean? What do you think? Means we're sick of white people getting in our faces."

"You're white."

"I am not white," Ricki shot back, hands on her hips. "I got an Afro, don't I? Just like Michael Jackson. And Liberty ain't white so that means I ain't white. I'm big as a bear, black as a crow, make more noise than the radio."

"That part's true," Isra mumbled. "Think we'll get a TV ?"

"No. Liberty don't like too many white people in the house, that's why she's listening to the radio all the time."

"White people on the radio."

"Yeah, but you can't see them."

"What's school going to be like?"

"Like kindergarten, only longer."

"Want to give me a peace sign tattoo?"

They started first grade at Mann Elementary School, carrying new lunch boxes and new pencils. They cried to have pierced ears but Liberty said no. Slaves had their ears pierced, like the way dogs have collars, so white people could tell who they belonged to. Her children were nobodies' slaves.

"But yours," Ricki said resentfully, crossing her arms.

"That's it, Rickshaw Jones. No records for a week."

"But—"

"No buts about it. Now get in your room before I throw you there."

Liberty sighed in exasperation. Busing home from work with two kids trailing behind, she was exhausted. *Well, now, Ricki can sit in her room for half an hour and just think on it. If I could just get her to concentrate on dancing or schoolwork instead of putting on fifteen thousand records as soon as she walks in the door, maybe then she'd be easier to handle. If anyone had told me raising children was going to be like this, I'd've raised minks instead.*

Tuesday morning meant the twins had a hot breakfast; that is, Isra had Cheerios and Rickshaw ate the oatmeal Liberty made, smacking her lips and gurgling with it in her mouth.

"You are gross," Isra said.

Ricki opened her full mouth.

"Liberty!"

"Cut it out, Ricki. And you, Isra, don't be a snitch."

Finally, she got them out of the house to school and took a long bath, stretching into the hot water and quiet. *How I love this. If there is a heaven, I hope it will be a big bathtub full of water with a pot of tea within reach.*

Terry Cee showed up at noon.

"You're early," Liberty said, holding the door open for him.

"Nice to see you, too. Where are my girls?"

"School. How's Billy Wayne?"

"Not so good. Doctors at the vet hospital still can't figure out what's wrong with him. Now he says he's no good in bed but to keep the sheets down."

"At least he's still got his sense of humor."

"Yeah," Terry nodded, fingering the love beads that hung around his neck.

"Your grin gets any bigger, you're going to split your head in half. What is it?"

He turned around. "Guess."

"Well," she surveyed him critically. "You didn't buy new clothes, because you'd be wearing them."

Terry looked at his clothing. "What's wrong with this?"

The boy must be legally blind, she thought. "Let's see. You changed color."

"Guess again."

"I hate these games."

"Come on."

"You found Jesus."

"Would I be standing in this house of sin if I did? Try again."

"You've been drafted."

"Hell no!" He shook his head. "I ain't going to Vietnam."

"I give up."

"One more."

"No. I told you, I hate this game. I hate it when my kids do it and now a grown man of eighteen years old is wasting my time. I've got to do my nails."

"Wait Liberty."

"Turn off the radio and put on a record, will you? My nerves need soothing."

"Liberty, wait—"

"I got an old Sam Cooke record there, put that on."

"Liberty come back, I said I'd tell you."

She walked back to the living room. "Well?"

"First, tomorrow night's the last night for me with the band." He looked at Liberty and chuckled.

"That's it? You're looking mighty pleased with yourself over that."

"I got in." He grabbed her hands. "I got accepted to the University. I start on September twenty-third. It's a Wednesday. I'm going to college, Liberty Grace."

She stared at him.

"I did it," he laughed. "I got in!"

"Terrence Wayne Clark," she hugged him as tight as she could. You did want this, didn't you? Good for you.

"Now, I won't be a regular student because I didn't finish high school, but I'm in. I can study anything I want, music, philosophy. Maybe I'll be a professor."

"Or one of those rich lawyers."

"I'm going to study composing, learn how to write all these tunes singing in my head." He grinned, his face shining. "Hell, maybe I'll be an undertaker—people dying to give me business."

"Ha." Liberty held him at arm's length. I've known him all his life and look at this surprise. "I'm proud of you, Terry."

He dug into the pocket of his vest and pulled out a worn savings account book. Twin City Federal was stamped in gold on the creased brown leatherette. "Take a look."

She opened it slowly. The first date, May 25, 1964, showed a deposit of twelve dollars and fifty-eight cents.

"Look at the end," he said, grabbing the book out of her hands and flipping the pages. "Right there."

"Twelve hundred seventy-two dollars and twenty-five cents." Liberty sat stunned.

"Three years. One-night stands, playing after-hours joints, rock dances at fraternities. Do you hear that song?" he asked suddenly. " 'You Can't Hurry Love,' Diana Ross and The Supremes, number six on the charts and still climbing, man. Some day, I swear, I'm going to be jamming with the Funk Brothers at Motown, look out." He clapped his hands together. "Can you believe it?"

"Why don't we go over to St. Paul, I'll put my paycheck in the bank, and you," she slapped the bank book against his thin chest, "can get a new one of these books. Then I'm taking you to lunch, anywhere you want to go."

He grinned. "I got a better idea. Why don't I take you to dinner tonight, someplace classy."

"You, spend money?" she hooted a laugh.

"Okay. I'll let you pay half."

She laughed at him again, the sudden tears misting her eyes. "You're something, you know?"

"Got it from my daddy-o."

"Telling me."

"Hey, Liberty Grace, will you still love me when I'm a college graduate?"

"I don't know, you're pretty stuck on yourself as it is."

He cranked the radio in his Merc as soon as he climbed in. Liberty and Terry shouted their laughter all the way to Anderhazy's, so loud everybody on the streets and in the other cars stared as they roared by. Driving as only a young man who's just won his first battle can drive, Terry skipped in and out of traffic, tapping the car door with his palm through the open window and hitting the horn for the sheer joy of the noise. He drove just as attention-getting over the bridge to the bank on Snelling and Randolph.

Terry turned off the ignition. "I'll get a new passbook while you do your thing, dig me?"

"Right on, bro," she sassed back.

We can have plenty of fun with this, she thought after depositing her paycheck and tucking the three tens and a twenty into her purse. "Excuse me," she said to a young white woman walking by, "Have you seen—"

"Your son is over there," the woman nodded in the other direction.

Liberty turned back to ask where, but the woman was gone. "Thank you, honky," she muttered, stepping around the columns and craning her neck. Amazing how quick those words come when you get angry. She shook her head. There he is, sitting in an office.

"Hey, Terry," she said, walking in and putting a hand on his shoulder.

He said nothing, just stared at the slips in front of him.

"Terry Cee?" Liberty asked, glancing from him to the white man behind the desk. His face was pink and a layer of fat hung over his collar, almost touching his tie.

"It's gone," Terry said huskily, as if his voice had dropped like an elevator to his feet.

"What?"

"It's all gone."

Liberty grabbed the withdrawal slips and thumbed through them.

"Are you the boy's mother?" the white man asked.

"Where's his money?" she asked between her teeth.

The banker let a smile pass over his face and fall off the edge. "His account was closed with a zero balance."

Rita, she knew instantly.

"I didn't take it, Liberty. I was getting some money for tonight, for dinner. See, look at my book," he urged, handing it to her.

"As I explained to Terrence, the co-signer of the account withdrew the balance yesterday. Now," the banker inhaled heavily, "we could go over the transactions again—"

"No," Terry interrupted. "No. Thank you."

Liberty followed him through the lobby to the doors and out into the spring sunshine. Shame, shame, she thought, that Rita, shooting her boy's money right into her arm. Liberty touched Terry's elbow as he opened the passenger side door for her. "Baby—"

She stopped. By his face she knew he wasn't listening to anything but his own thoughts buzzing like a thousand bees caught in a jar. Oh, Terry, we got to figure something out for you. We'll think of something. Liberty glanced out the window as St. Paul became Minneapolis at the Lake Street Bridge, the car quiet but for the Ike and Tina Turner Revue playing on the radio.

"Isra?"

She spun around. For a moment, her eyes were unfocused. "Ricki?"

"How is she? Can I see her?"

"Ricki." She hugged her twin sister tightly. Through their clothes, she could feel the sameness of their bodies, the long-waisted thinness, strong backs. How much the same and how different we are. Ricki. Big sister. Untouchable and hugging her like the children they were.

"Take it easy," Ricki whispered. She rubbed her sister's back with her hand. "How bad is she?"

Isra stepped away. "Very."

"When can I see her?"

"At the top of the hour. For five minutes."

"Five minutes?"

Isra nodded.

"If Liberty knew that, she would flip right out. Is she feeling any pain?"

Ricki, always the big sister. "They don't know. The nurse says she's got to rest and they'll know more after she wakes up. If she wakes up." Isra's burning eyes filled with tears again, scalding her vision.

"She going to die?" Ricki laid her hands on Isra's shoulders. Tense. Too tense, hardly feels like Isra, she'd never let herself get this wired.

"I don't know," her sister answered softly.

"You think so, don't you?"

Isra nodded her head once. Yes, she wanted to shout. Yes, she's going to die and we'll be left alone, Ricki. We'll be alone.

Someone beckoned from the nurses' station.

"Come on," Isra said.

Ricki followed her down the corridor. White, she thought, perfectly sterile, makes me want to die looking at walls with no color on them. Isra slowed at a doorway and stepped into a small cubicle. Ricki glanced around. On a small table sat a vase with two red roses barely open, and machines with wires and beeps and lights filled the room. She followed one wire with her eyes as it snaked across the floor and under the bed. All these machines got wheels attached, she noticed. They all got little wheels.

Isra moved closer to the bed. "Ricki," she whispered, lifting Liberty's hand.

Ricki didn't move. All God's machines got wheels.

"Rickshaw." Isra stared at her. Get over here, me and you got to pull Liberty back to shore. Isra shook her head quickly, her mind feeling scrambled. She glanced up, hearing Ricki's boots scraping the linoleum floor.

Ricki stepped to the other side of the bed, still not looking at Liberty's face. The hand resting on the sheet had an IV taped to the back, the white gauze startling as it netted the creases in Liberty's skin. Gently, so as not to hurt her or loosen the tube, Ricki laced her fingers through her mother's.

"Liberty," Israellen said, leaning over the bed. "Rickshaw's here."

Ricki squeezed Liberty's fingers. Slowly, she traced her hand to her wrist, up her thin arm to her shoulder. She inhaled sharply. Look at everything one by one then look at her whole face. Loose skin around her neck, a small dry patch on her cheek, maybe she scraped her face when she fell, Ricki thought. Her jaw hung open and her cheeks seemed narrower. Her eyelids were thin, damp and very still. No movement from her eyes; she wasn't dreaming, wasn't thinking, just lying there, breathing. The lines in her forehead and the wrinkles around her eyes seemed deeper, as if they had dug more of her away when she wasn't looking. There's less of her than before, Ricki decided. She's disappearing like the Cheshire cat.

"Ricki?"

Rickshaw blinked suddenly, aware that she was sweating. "You all right?"

She nodded and licked her lips. "Long trip from Waco."

Back in the waiting room, Israellen sat down on the couch. Let Ricki do some of the pacing, she thought, exhausted.

Her sister looked down at her. "What happened?"

Isra sighed. "I don't know. Madame called me from Anderhazy's, said Liberty had collapsed."

Ricki nodded, then turned away to look out the window. "What are you doing here, Isra?" she asked, her voice almost dreamy in the quiet, dim room. "Who would come to Minneapolis during winter?"

Israellen blinked her eyes. What is she talking about? "I

have some news. I'm getting married. I thought Liberty would want to hear about it from me."

"Where's your boyfriend?"

Why won't Ricki look at me, Isra thought suddenly. "Caleb's still in England. He's very busy. I wanted to visit Liberty anyway and I had some time—"

"What about your school?" Ricki interrupted. "Liberty said you were going to school."

"I'm dropping out."

"Dropping out," Ricki said softly, then turned from the window, "To get married. Anything else?"

"I don't appreciate you acting like this."

"Acting like what?"

"Acting like I gave Liberty a heart attack." Isra stood up to face her sister. "Why are you blaming me?"

"I never said I was blaming you."

"No, but you will."

Ricki turned away again. Israellen reached out her hand to touch Ricki's back, then stopped. Already, like a hand finally closing into a fist, she has shut me out.

The wind blasted Ricki as she struggled up the sand dune. Grabbing fistfuls of sand as if it was a magic rope, she made it to the top. Her lungs ached and the wind rushed through her clothes and hair. Some people think that if you mourn the dead too much, the dead can't move onto the next stage. Transmigration or reincarnation or some other such word. If that's true, maybe it's best to live by yourself; then no one can catch you in a web of sadness. Except denying satisfaction makes you itchy and you'll spend all your time explaining to yourself why you're alone. Maybe you'll have nobody's sadness to tie you to the earth, but your life will be full of lost time and empty space. Is that what I think? Is it what I fear?

There, on the next dune she could see her twin sister looking out to sea. "Isra!" she shouted, joy threading her voice. "Israellen!"

179

Five

Ricki's knees jolted at the bottom of the next dune. She gritted her teeth, sweat stinging her eyes and began the hard run uphill. The sand closed around her feet like a pair of thousand-fingered hands wanting to pull her in. She pumped her legs and leaned forward, shoving so hard against the dune her thighs and ankles ached with effort. Push. Come on, push. She squeezed her eyes shut and felt the rush of strength to her muscles.

Spring came to the city. Dogs ran for no reason but to run, jump ropes came out, and while everyone wore their winter coats in the morning, they carried them home in the afternoon. Saturdays, Ricki would take her shoes off to see if it was warm enough yet to go barefoot, and twice already she stepped on thawing dogshit in the yard. Moist winds promised summer.

It was Tuesday. The twins raced each other from Mann School. Ricki won the race, but it didn't matter; Isra had an A+ spelling test that Liberty would stick to the refrigerator with a magnet while Ricki sulked, her test hidden under the stack of mail on the coffee table.

The evening grew darker and colder. Huey's mom called him in. They were up on Fifth Avenue studying an anthill between the cement squares of the sidewalk when they heard Liberty finally call.

"What's for dinner?" Ricki shouted, as they busted in. "Liberty?"

Liberty sat in her chair, staring at nothing. The twins walked up to her.

"Liberty?" Ricki asked again, a little doubtful.

She looked up at the two of them. They're growing up, she realized, they're growing up and out of my house. "Sit down," she said, her voice like gravel.

The twins shared a look and sat on the couch.

"Listen," she said in the same voice, standing up and walking across the room. "Listen to the radio."

With shaking fingers she turned up the volume. The voice on the speakers was flat and precise, and had no trace of a Tennessee accent, which was where the newscaster was reporting from. Memphis, he said, at a place called the Lorraine Motel. Ten minutes before, only ten minutes, a bullet had struck Martin Luther King Junior as he stood on a balcony. Now they're waiting for further reports.

"Did you hear?" Liberty asked. There was an edge in the way she talked as if her mind was stumbling and the sound of her voice was the only thing keeping her upright. Deep in her chest, Liberty felt her heart shimmy, out-of-beat. "Did you hear?"

"Dr. King is dead?" Isra asked.

"Not yet, he's not dead yet."

"But he will be," Ricki said.

"Yes," Liberty nodded, looking past them and out the window. She could see cars moving slowly down Fifth Avenue, driving beyond Banfield Street and all the people living there.

"He got shot," Isra said.

"Yes."

"No reason for anybody to shoot him," Ricki observed.

"No reason for anybody to shoot anybody," Isra replied.

Sadness welled up in Liberty. Like all the pain had sunk into the ground, she thought, and has to rise up now as if stretching its hands to caress my face.

"They shot him because he's black," Ricki said flatly.

"They shot him because he didn't do what they said," Isra countered.

"Who are they?" Liberty asked.

"White people," Ricki answered quickly.

"Bad people," Israellen corrected.

"Same thing," Rickshaw shot back, wondering if she should wipe the slow tears from her mother's face.

"No, baby, not the same," Liberty whispered.

The room darkened as night came. The neighborhood grew as quiet as the house on Banfield Street. Isra and Ricki made sandwiches, even one with extra grape jelly for Liberty, which she didn't touch. Rickshaw turned the radio back on, long enough to hear that King had died and announcers begging people to stay home, listen to James Brown and stay out of the streets. It was no time for violence or riots or demonstrations, they would betray his dream of peace.

Liberty watched them, not moving from her chair as her twins ate their sandwiches. Dreams are as good as using spiderwebs against a flood, Liberty thought. All this talk of dreams. Dreams Mamie forgot as she was dying and Cherise tried to believe in. Dreams Emma chases like shadows. Dreams gone wrong, bitter like cold coffee in the morning, they cut slashes down my children's faces so when I look at them I see nothing but scars running from forehead to chin. Forcing her body to relax, Liberty turned to stare out the front window, the dark canyon of the street staring back. How can I believe in a dream? A dream gone bad pulls the trigger of guns aimed at innocent people. A dream gone bad is the explosion of a bomb thrown into a church. How can I believe a bad dream won't take my children away someday? She looked down Banfield Street till she could make out small beads of light moving in the street.

"Rickshaw, Israellen! Hurry!"

They rushed out of their bedrooms.

"Get your coats!" Liberty jumped from her chair and reached for her sweater. There they were, not many and moving slowly.

She grabbed their hands and they raced up the street. Someone handed each of them a candle as they joined the marchers. Her two children walked next to her, Isra biting her lip as if that would make sure her small candle would not go out, and Ricki looking around, her face and eyes the color of flame. Like a necklace, she thought glancing around her. We are a tangled necklace of light in the soft spring night. A man in the front sang out a sermon, while the people around Liberty and her daughters cried out Amens.

I have no amen to call out, Liberty thought. I've got no words to cry out in the nighttime. He's dead now, a proud black man who lived his life in the cross hairs of a rifle scope, the last peaceful hope. In the morning, rage will boil over into the streets my children walk to school and I have no amen to defend them with. Her loss made her ache—her arms, her breasts, making her single thoughts sharp enough to hurt. I'm not in Memphis, but why does Memphis seem like the world right now? Walking from under the light of a streetlamp, Liberty could see the small pinpricks of stars in the sky. I could shout so loud each star would hear it. I could give the brightest of them each a name, turn each point of light into a memory. Memories. I have my twins and my memories.

"I remember, I remember," Liberty called as warm wax melted down the side of the candle and onto her fingertips, her voice melding with the sobs and voices and footfalls around her. I always remember and hope. Emma Nevada, please be safe. Let this light reach you.

The whitewashed church building was too small to hold all of them but the deacon had offered it first and the marchers followed him. They filed in slowly, silence rippling over them like water. Liberty didn't hear the pleading from the ministers to keep peace. She sat in the folding chair staring out a single small open window at a star pulsing to its own beat.

Oh, Freedom, Oh, Freedom / Oh, Freedom over me…

Liberty heard the voice of her clumsy daughter, Ricki, singing songs she herself could only remember pieces of. Cherise had sung the same song as she scrubbed the soiled linen and colostomy pads in the washtub full of hot water and Borax that made her skin dry out and flake if she didn't cover them with grease.

And before I'll be a slave / I'll be buried in my grave / And go home to my Lord and be free...

Now, singing full and clear, her not-yet-eight-year-old with gold skin and emerald eyes lifted up the words and sent them to the sky.

Isra heard her name ricochet off the sand dunes. A strong breeze rippled through her hair and roared around her ears. There, a thin gray line between the sand and the sky. The ocean. The Atlantic. I love water. Once, at Hyde Park, the Serpentine became so still that the sky and the trees lit up the pond like another world and it was easy to believe that Alice could've gone through the looking glass just as Angel believed. I love the sea and how the sky seems to carry the moods of it all over this island.

Isra looked out the living room window of the house on Banfield Street. The clouds appeared solid as it rained, making the ground look unsteady.

"I don't know. Liberty wasn't raised by her biological parents." Isra walked over to the recliner and sat down, suddenly struck with how little she knew about the woman who had raised her.

"How about her adoptive parents?"

"One died of cancer. Colon cancer." She glanced out again. There had been a window at the crematorium, too. Isra had stared out as long as she could, squeezing Caleb's hand, repeating over and over, there is good that will come of this. There is some good. Once, just once, she met Ricki's eyes as they stood in that horrible place, the box holding Liberty between them. I wonder if Ricki will climb the water tower to sing to God about this. Probably, even though Liberty didn't believe in God.

"I never said I didn't believe in God," Liberty explained to the Seventh-Day Adventist with his foot in the door. "I just don't understand why people praise Christ like he was a brand new Cadillac with shiny chrome and whitewalls. Amen, let's ride the Jesus Express right into downtown Salvation, hallelujah."

"And I can't remember how the other died," Isra said slowly, aware she was lying. People can die of a broken heart because Cherise did, Liberty told us. I remember it clear as that window. Did Liberty's heart get broken? Did I break it? Is Ricki right?

The woman accepted a ten-dollar donation for the Heart Association and left. Isra sank back into the recliner chair. One week and already I can feel myself turning into Liberty just as sure as she turned to ash. She shook her head and glanced at her watch. Caleb is home now. His suitcase is by the door, his coat thrown over the settee and he probably managed to kick off his shoes before curling up with the rest of his clothes on. Soon, love. I'll be home soon. "Soon," she whispered in the empty room, concentrating on sending it over the ocean to him.

Sitting on this beach, years after falling in and out of love, I feel like I'm farther away from him than if I'd never met him. But he's not a stranger to me. Maybe that's what's wrong. Maybe if I didn't know him I could want him again. Instead, we live so close in that flat, so close but never touching, only reflecting one another like the sky and the sea. It seems what stands between us is a one-way mirror and I used to want to scream at him to look at me. Look at me, at everything I am and everything I used to be and still wish for. How far away he seems now. How far away they all are. Liberty, Emma, Ricki.

Rebecca married Tick, Bobby Harris's brother. He gave her a ring, a one-bedroom apartment, a baby and a broken arm. Her letters stopped coming after that, as if she couldn't share any more of her life with me, but had to save it all up to get away from him.

"Bobby Harris is a creep, Isra." Ricki's whisper was sharp in the small bathroom, its urgency bouncing off the tiled walls.

"What would you know about men anyway?"

"He's married and he's running around. Isn't that enough?"

Isra splashed water over her face. "I'm not in love with him."

"Then what are you doing with him?"

"Just having a good time."

"Did you fuck him?"

"Shut up, Rickshaw." She reached for a hand towel and dried her face.

"Did you?"

"None of your business."

"You're my sister."

"That's right. Your sister. Not your kid, not your dog, not one of your goddamn lezzie friends following you everywhere."

"You were afterhours at Johnny's with five men, drunk off your ass. You were asking for trouble."

Liberty stared through the barely open door, the air seeming lethal with tension. "That's enough. I don't want to hear any more from either one of you. Ricki, are you going grocery shopping or not?"

Ricki looked at her twin once more then whirled on her heel and out the door.

"Why don't you make some coffee, Isra?" she asked, settling into her chair with the Sunday paper. What has happened to them? They just don't act like they used to. Once they kept each other's secrets, now they never talk but to fight. I never thought I'd see it.

She opened the paper. Isra's sleeping with some man Ricki doesn't approve of. Be nice if I'd at least been introduced to him. Been nice if Ricki hadn't made such a racket pushing Isra through the basement window to get her inside last night. Been nice if one or the other would've called to let me know where they were and not to worry. I'd've worried anyway no matter where they were, but not hearing I always assume they are in the worst places, which they were. At least Ricki got her out of there. And Isra drinking. Drinking away her loss, like Mamie. Did Mamie rub off on me enough that I passed it on to my child? My little girl, my ballerina, my stringbean, my daughter, am I going to lose you like that?

Liberty smoothed the newspaper, realizing she hadn't read a word. What do I do? Wait. Wait it out, hope she's all right. Ricki will look after her, as long as Isra doesn't push her so far away they can't find one another again. Liberty let the paper fall to her lap. Oh, God, if there's anything I wish it's for my daughters not to lose each other. Emma Nevada, I am counting on your unseen influence on my children.

"You live alone, Emma. Are you lonely?"

Emma pulled another weed out of the garden. "I don't live alone, now, honey. I live with you. Watch out, that's a carrot you're pulling."

Isra let go of the green stem. "But are you lonely other times?"

"Every now and then." Emma brushed Isra's cheek with her hand. Her fingers were warm and smelled of earth and soap. "Most times I'm happy all by myself."

"Which most, lonely or happy?"

"Happy." Emma dropped her hand. "Are you lonely, honey?"

Isra shrugged and picked up a small hand shovel. "Sometimes."

"You got Ricki. And your mama."

"I know." Isra dug a thin trench.

"What are you doing to my broccoli, girl?"

"Digging a little trench for the animals."

Emma laughed for some time. "You like animals?"

"Uh huh. But we don't got any living here with us."

Then Emma got me Queenie the turtle. Maybe that's what I need now, trade Caleb in for a dog or a cat, Isra thought, walking through Waterloo Station to the bus stop. She got in the queue behind an old woman wearing a black hat with a veil and glanced at the others standing around her. Ordinary people. How can they stand it? Do they love their jobs like I love acting? Do they love their children instead? Do they masquerade at work and become themselves when they get home or to the pub?

A bus rolled to a halt in front of them and Isra waited patiently for her turn to get on. What a funny city this is. People actually stand in line to get on the bus and make way for the old people. She climbed the stairs and chose a seat in the back. I love that smell, she thought, inhaling the cigarette smoke and the dampness. Isra glanced out the window as a group of young American tourists gawked at a monument. Two seats ahead of her sat a young white woman smoking, her hair bleached almost to green and her Wimpy uniform stark orange. A regular job. Fabulous. Go work at a Wimpy, end up a little crazy, live in this big city with three cats, misering away all my money and living in a little bed-sit. When I die, they'll find three million pounds in a box under my bed, like the lady in the *Guinness Book of World Records* who was so stingy she saved soap slivers.

Isra slumped down in her seat. I feel like a kitten tied up in a burlap bag about to be thrown into a pond. She tried to push back the feeling. Ever since Liberty died, fear has layered onto me, deflecting all the world could give or comfort me with. Now that fear is unraveling like yarn, leaving me exposed and wanting to crawl under the seat because of the newness of my skin. And everyone around me—the driver, the riders, the people on the sidewalk, all of them—is wrapped in my fear.

She squeezed her eyes shut. Why am I so afraid? Why do I feel like this when I have Caleb? What a good man and he has such a face—how could such a face happen by chance? A sculptor must've carved it and a miracle brought it to life. It's not his fault I feel somehow—she stopped the thought right there. Cut it out, Isra. Think about the play, think about the flat, think about Theatre of Panic, think of anything but you and Caleb. Brooding only makes it worse. I spent my life in a city where brooding is the most common activity. Six, seven, eight months of winter can turn a woman into herself.

Squeezing her fists and opening her eyes, she looked out the window again. A big city like London, so many people, how can I be alone? I have Caleb. She could see his silver blond hair that hung to his shoulders, almost feel his thin chest. He is too thin. He worries everything off. I wonder if he worries about us? I wonder if he knows this uneasiness I feel, wonder if he's ever been left to brood. Isra relaxed her hands and ran them over her face. They smelled like dust. Holding her hands open in front of her, she stared at her palms, the creases dark like braids of maple syrup. "I'm lonely," she murmured, then glanced around quickly to see if anyone heard.

No one looked at her or even tilted a head in her direction to listen better. I'm talking aloud on the bus, I must be going around the bend. Harold Pinter says that speech is a constant stratagem to cover nakedness. Maybe those quiet little words have just covered the parts of me that are exposed. Isra smiled sadly. In the window she could see the reflection of her mouth and chin against the colors of London. But I am lonely. I miss them; I let Liberty and Rickshaw drop right out of my hands.

The sand dunes were gold in the late evening sun that turned the small hairs along the back of Isra's wrists into translucent gold wire. She inhaled deeply. Seaweed, she thought, and something else. It's always something else. Clouds crowding into the sun, love crowding into art. Now Caleb, crowding into my mind, into myself. Sex and race, he used to say, make no difference. I used to think that was his saving grace but now I wonder. Who is he to erase that I am a woman and that I am black? Who is he to ignore my heritage and my strength?

"Hi." Ricki looked around the beach.

"Hi," Isra said quietly.

"It's beautiful."

"Yeah."

"Should we go down there and spoil it?"

They followed the steep trail and headed for an outcropping of rock.

"Did you ever miss that?" Isra asked, nodding at a picnicking family. "Mom, dad, aunts, uncles, that stuff."

"Naw. I had Liberty, and you, and Emma, and all sorts of other people."

"And music."

"Yeah. Music."

"I don't think it's the same for me. I mean, your music is the most important thing—"

"One of the most important things, baby sister," Ricki corrected. "Just one."

"One of the most important things. But my work doesn't feel like that. Dancing used to, I mean, I could sink into it right up to my neck. But not acting. It's like trying to learn to swim but there's only a puddle to practice in."

"And you want to be in the sea."

Israellen grasped Ricki's hand in answer.

"Careful, baby sister. Those people have been looking at us funny since we got here."

Isra grinned. Both knew just how often people missed that they were sisters, much less twins. Ever since high school, when Ricki got further into jeans and leather and Isra's clothes got closer to neon. But Isra knew their sameness. She had always known it. Some days she'd get out of bed, toes curling against the cold floor and swipe Ricki's boots and t-shirt. How easily she could copy her sister. The clothes seemed to cover more than just her body against the cold autumn morning, seemed to erase everything she had put between them to show how different they were. Ricki's sullen attitude fit her as well as her boots. Just wearing them makes me feel hard, Isra decided, studying the mirror. There's already a sneer on my face.

Rebecca honked again, the foghorn of her Delta 88 the only part of the car that worked right.

"Get your butt outside and tell that girl to stop making such a racket, Isra," Liberty commanded, swinging into the bathroom holding her ratty bathrobe shut with one hand.

Ricki stormed out of her room, barefoot and shirtless, her hair sticking flat to her head. "Give them back."

"Put a shirt on, girl, and get the hell out of this house."

Isra ducked around Liberty and past Ricki. "I'll be home late," she called over her shoulder, scooping up her books and Ricki's jean jacket. "Extra workout. Don't wait dinner."

Her mother and her sister heard the front door slam.

"Well?" Liberty asked, feeling tired and sick of her sixteen-year-olds.

"Well what?"

"You better get dressed and start walking or you'll be late again."

"I ain't."

"Ain't? What sort of way to talk is that?"

"Ain't is a word; it's in the dictionary. And I ain't going to school. I'm sick. Caught a cold standing here in this unheated house with my tits humming in the wind." Her bedroom door slammed shut.

Damn Rickshaw, won't listen to anybody. Sets herself to something and tunes out the rest of the world by disappearing into her head. Liberty opened the bedroom door. Ricki sat in the middle of the unmade bed, earphones plugged into her amp and eyes squeezed shut. Hasn't even put a shirt on,

Liberty thought, closing the door. One daughter a musician and one daughter a dancer equals two broke always. She walked down the hall to the living room. And now Ricki wants to quit school. I can't let her do that, no matter how bad we fight. She's not dumb, just can't seem to get her schoolwork finished. Would help if she concentrated on it more and her guitar less but music is what she wants. She has a right to want what she wants. At least I have no problems with Isra. She knows dancing requires discipline and school is just another exercise. Besides, it comes easy to her; it seems Isra got all the grace and brains they were supposed to share. What did Ricki get? The ability to listen. She can really listen. She can hear some things most people think are in their imaginations. I believe both will see it as equal when they're older.

Liberty studied the framed photograph on the mantle. It was taken at the playground just before the twins turned eight. Isra stood in front, her smile perfect, the Hollywood child. And Ricki in back, the slight dimple that appears above her eyebrow when she is frowning showing in her forehead. Though the picture was only of their faces, Liberty was sure Ricki's hand, out of camera range, was wrapped firmly around Isra's wrist to lead her away.

She'll do what I say, Ricki thought, peeping around the locker room at Anderhazy's. "Don't change," she whispered to her sister.

"What?"

"Don't put your leotard on."

"We'll be late."

"Come on." Ricki walked away.

Isra glanced around then stashed her dance clothes back in her bag.

Ricki could reach the window if she stood on the back of the toilet in the third stall. She scrambled onto the sill and pushed the glass hard to open the window. The drop below was high, but not too high, she decided. "You coming or not?"

"Coming where? We're late."

"No, we're not. We're absent." Ricki grinned from the window. "What's the matter?"

"I don't want to."

"You afraid?"

"No." Isra glanced at the cracked tiles of the bathroom floor. The black stuff between them always gave her a twinge in her stomach. "I like it."

"You like it?"

"I like ballet dancing."

Ricki stared. Ballet was horrible, all the girls and the two boys standing in front of mirrors with one hand on the barre as Madame screeched out numbers, her knees sticking out like apples under her dance skirt. Her voice was croaky and she spoke with an accent like someone in the movies. Bet that's where she got it, Ricki thought.

But Isra loved her. She loved Madame's old shawl that she took off to show a position. She loved the pink and black leotards, the music and the picture of her, Israellen Jones, in the huge mirrors that stretched to the ceiling. Because I am good. Madame knows I am good. "I'm staying."

Isra socked Ricki on the arm. "Race you to that rock," she shouted, tearing across the beach.

Six

Ricki ran behind, watching Isra race across the sand, tears edging into her eyes. She is so beautiful. Never seen anything like that, never seen how much someone I love can show me how much beauty there is. Maybe this is to be her fortune in life; to show, just by being her, what beauty can be. Maybe dancing wasn't for her after all. But for so long that was how it was, that was the way it was supposed to be. Our lives were supposed to be as braided as dancing and music. Maybe we wouldn't have broken apart if she had stayed a dancer, something I could understand. Maybe she wouldn't have been lost. But it doesn't matter now. We've come back to each other, two broken pieces together again.

At the rock, they both stood gulping down air. Isra bent over her legs, her long hair swinging almost to the sand and her pulse pounding in her temples.

"I'll climb up first, then give you a hand, okay?" Ricki asked, hooking the bag over her shoulder.

"In a minute," Isra said, turning towards the sea. I love the ocean. I wish I could gather it up in my arms. I want to stand hip-deep in it, feeling sand and stones beneath my feet. I want to shout how much I love the water as loudly as the waves and carry it in my hair so when I stand offstage waiting for my cue, I catch the scent and grin. I want to be as strong, as knowing, as sure in anger and calm. Caleb said I want life to be like a movie.

"Not worrying about details like clothes or the shape of the room or integrity. All you think of is the lines you say and the slant of the light on your pretty face. But this life isn't a movie, Isra, so stop acting." He got out of their bed, his words replacing the touch of his skin.

She walked slowly to the line of the waves. Every one of his words grated against the softest parts of me, wearing me away. Even after our worst fights, even when I was in such a fury, I thought I'd burst into fire if his arm brushed my breast or I could smell his hair, all of me turned to him, defeating my anger. Till those words, each like a grain of sand, scraped away the sharp lines between what was good and should be remembered, and what was bad and should be forgotten.

Ricki climbed up the face of the rock to a ledge and sat down. Gulls and sailboats silhouetted against the sun. The water followed the sky in color, a ribbon of gold and orange and lipstick-red followed by a broad sash of green-blue and navy. The seasons are written into water, she thought. Humidity turning the horizon white in summer, the spring-green streams ready to jump their beds, metal-gray autumn creeks. And the ice, ice so white it's blue in winter. I took living on the road instead of choosing the water, the hard-cider smell of fall, and the leaves bursting with color. There's no escaping the way things feel in the North—with the end of the leaves turning, autumn turns into itself and leaves people to do the same. The cold rain, the sullen creeks and the bird nests look like tangled hair caught in the bare trees. And I brood, waiting for winter and dazzling blue skies that seep into the shadows thrown by a weak winter sun. I brood and wait for the blues.

"Yaz says I can't play the blues." Ricki stared at the melting ice cubes in her water glass. The waitress had long since stopped filling it and she was suddenly thirsty again. "He says I don't have my own sound because I don't have my own sadness."

Angel dragged a finger across the back of Ricki's hand. "What's that mean?"

"I only got general sadness, like people starving to death and war and stuff like that, not sadness of my own. He says what I got to be blue about is nothing compared to one word from Miss Bessie or Ida May Cox. I got nothing to sing out of myself."

"You think he's right?"

She shrugged. "Maybe I don't got a no-good man beating me every Friday, maybe I've never been really poor and had no way to get out, but you don't have to be broke to be schooled in the blues. Like you don't have to look black to signify black."

Angel sipped from her water glass.

"I can do things with sounds. I can hear differences, I can hear how Billie Holiday says yes, and I can tell hers from Minnie Ripperton's or Dinah Washington's or Bessie's. I learned Bessie's first. There ain't nobody who can say yes like Bessie Smith says yes."

The waitress came by with the check resting under two fortune cookies. Ricki chose one, Angel the other.

"I don't want to sit in places like Johnny's all my life playing to nobody."

Angel put her cookie on the table where it sat gold and curved against the white tablecloth. "Do you believe in these things?"

Ricki shook her head.

With one fist, Angel smashed the fortune cookie to bits then pulled out a small white slip of paper. "Too bad."

Ricki leaned the bag against her calves. She shook back her dreadlocks, the cool ocean air calming her by the second. Angel believed in luck. I think I believe in it, too. Some people have luck that carries them forever, good or bad, like Isra. Others have it come and go, like it's stuck to a wheel that's spun by someone else's hand, like me. And others use up all their good fortune in the first years of their lives, leaving nothing to protect them.

That Rita. She's just born to be bad luck. Liberty slapped her new Billie Holiday record onto the turntable and settled into her chair. After work today, Liberty's leg ached so much she limped home from the bus stop. But there was another ache that had nothing to do with the season. Poor Terry Cee, she thought, pinching her lower lip between her fingers. She'd invited him in yesterday afternoon but he just said no, his face the same smooth blank it was since they'd left the bank. Liberty sighed and moved her leg slowly. The damp thawing winds made her hurt. Why do I stay here? she thought.

I don't know why, when I'm feeling so sad...

What a day. I hate it when a person can't tell if it's spring or fall by the weather. That always means it's a cold rain and a cold wind and that miserable gray sky. All the dampness of spring is painful enough without this. At least the twins aren't home yet to harass me. Will be in a minute, unless Ricki gets detention again. Whoever heard of a first grader getting detention? There was a knock at the door. Wonder who that is, she thought, getting up stiffly. Probably Montgomery Wards with my order.

I long to try something I've never had...

"Terry Cee," she said in surprise, opening the door for him. She looked him over, from his neat Afro to his sandals, lingering only at his face and at the guitar case he held in one hand.

Never had no kissing...

"Come on in," she said. "Going to take me up on the offer to talk? Let me get you a beer." She limped into the kitchen.

Terry followed her in, then stood in the living room to stare out the front windows. "Leg bothering you, huh?"

Oh, what I've been missing...

"Always does this time of year," she answered, coming back with a can. "Here. Looks like you could use something a little stronger."

Lover man, oh where can you be?...

"So sit down," she said, "Or at least turn around so I can see your face."

He shuffled around to face her. "I joined up."

The night is cold and I'm so all alone...

She froze. "What?"

"I joined the Marines. I leave in three days for boot camp."

I'd give my soul just to call you my own...

"You can't be serious."

"Yes ma'am, I am."

Got a moon above me...

"Terry, there is a war on."

But no one to love me...

"I know. You don't mind me turning this off, do you?"

Lover man, oh where can you be?...

She shook her head slowly. "Why did you join up?"

He lifted the needle from the record. "What choice do I have?"

"Terry, you are a musician, a good musician. You got your whole life ahead of you."

"Joining the Marines doesn't mean my life is over. Besides, it was enlist or get drafted. I wanted to have some say over my life."

"What if you get hurt?"

"I won't."

"I'll bet your daddy said the same thing. Have you told him yet?"

"I'm going to. After I leave here." He stared at her as if she was a puzzle he had to solve. "Where's your girl, where's Ricki? Thought she'd be home by now."

"So did I. They should come walking through the door any minute."

"She's always after me to let her play my guitar." Terry walked to the case lying on the floor and lifted it onto the sofa. He opened it slowly and touched the triangular dent on the front of the guitar. "Better not have another scratch on it when

I come back. This is a Fender Stratocaster, a hell of a guitar. You tell her that."

"Tell her yourself."

He closed the case and shook his head. "You do it, Liberty. She'll need another case in a year or so. I put duct tape on the bottom, she'll have to watch it. You tell little sister those things for me, you hear?"

Liberty got postcards later, telling about boot camp and the Black Power Movement sweeping the platoon. She sent him copies of *In a Silent Way*, *Quintet of the Hot Club of France*, *Aretha: Lady Soul* and *Electric Ladyland*, and wrote that they'd amputated so much of Billy Wayne because of his diabetes, he could almost fit on a skateboard. She didn't get a reply. In June, she listened to Senator Fulbright on the radio, looked up Hanoi in the atlas and prayed Terry Cee was a cook or a mechanic and not in anybody's line of fire.

Almost a year later an officer in a neatly pressed uniform knocked on the door of the house on Banfield Street, holding a foregone conclusion in the shape of a telegram. Liberty ordered him off her steps and out of her yard. The telegram she stuck on the kitchen wall with a thumbtack, leaving it to blow in the hot summer breezes.

Terry Cee's guitar was tuned the old way, open D, like for Tampa Red, Blind Willie, Bukka White and Robert Johnson. Now for Rickshaw Jones. She squinted against the stage lights at the audience, trying to find one old familiar face. Nothing. Not Nadine, not Tayla, she could see none of her old lovers. "The middle of the night is a blues thing. In the middle of the night, it's blues that cover you, keeping you warm and holding the smell of love against your skin. Those times when your bed gets too big because it's made for two and it's only sleeping one. And there's a nightmare just waiting to bite you in the neck, it's the blues that protects you. A long time ago, some people walked into my life. I listened to them so much, I thought for sure I was going to bust."

"Tell us, sugar," a voice cried out in the darkness.

"This is for Bessie. And Billie. And Ma Rainey." Good old Ma. Got to prove it on you, don't we? Ricki thought with a grin, reaching for the brass guitar slide and fitting it on her pinkie. She looked out at the audience again. "See, when I first started playing the blues, all I could hear was me making a mess. Then I fell in love—"

The audience erupted in understanding laughter.

"And love being love and me being me, well…" she trailed off. Just play, dammit. Talk doesn't mean anything.

The notes bent under her hands, harsh and hard and liquid sweet, like only the blues can be.

"This train is bound for glory, this train…" Liberty sang softly over and over. Like the needle got stuck in the record, she realized, stopping suddenly. The silence that fell around her made her want to shout to push it back. She took a deep breath. Sunshine burnt across the unkempt fields, filling them with so much light and heat, Liberty was sure her head would burst. Small geysers of dust whirled and settled in the bare patches of earth. A rusty mailbox perched on a gatepost, the gate long gone but for a curving ditch in its memory.

Henry's Chevy was parked off the dirt road across from Bub's house. A shotgun house, she decided, looking closely at more wood than paint showing. Sitting in the driver's seat, she felt dizzy. It's the sun, Liberty thought, and not sleeping for two days to drive down here. The heat seemed to wrap around her legs, and the dust in her shoes mixed with her sweat to turn her feet muddy. Just heat and kudzu choking life out of everything, even the air, and who knows who's hiding behind the next patch of scrub-oak. Might be some gun-toting redneck taking aim because it's open season year-round on snakes and niggers in McComb County, Mississippi.

Emma was right. I have no business here. Nineteen fifty-nine is no time for me to be sitting in a field waiting for some white man to make an accident happen. Leave it to Emma

Nevada to tell me what's safe and what isn't—she's off doing god knows what. She'll get herself killed and I'll read about it in the morning paper.

I have to get out of here. The hate floats in the air like pollen. Every breath pulls more into me. But I had to come down here, didn't I? It's not even my land, not even my house, but I had to see them, had to borrow Henry's car and sit in the dust staring at it. She wiped the sweat off her top lip. I'm going home, she decided. I got a home now, Bub and me saw to that. He couldn't just give me himself with all his kindness; had to give me a place of my own.

She started the Chevy and pulled away. Up ahead, two women walked down the narrow road, their dresses bright enough to throw the sun back into the sky. They don't even feel it, she realized, they don't even feel it.

The rock is still warm from the sun, Ricki realized, gripping the hard, worn stone tightly. She glanced at Isra down by the water. I let them go, Ricki thought. My home. My family. Let them slip away as easy as sand from a fist. She lifted her hands up. I must have my father's hands. I know I got Liberty's touch—her way of making things sing. For her it was her daughters, for Isra it's the air, for me it's my guitar and my lover's body. One lover. Just that one lover.

What had happened? I can remember aching at night after Angel left, no matter how hard I tried to forget, to sleep or to copy the touch of her with someone else. I fell in love with a woman who wanted no such thing. I fell for the only woman worth falling in love with other than Bessie Smith, who is more like a god than a person anyway.

For the first time, Ricki had realized the taste of the sun could fill her whole body and she could hear leaves whispering. Angel, she thought, walking down the city street as the wind caressed her hands and face. Angel, you are the second heart beating in my life. Ricki loved Bessie Smith, the blues, and now for the first time, her lover, a lover she knew to her fingertips she loved. The sun came up for them, Ricki's body unfolded like a ballet slipper to her touch. For the second time in her life, Ricki bought roses. The first had been 1975, for Liberty's birthday. She'd given her mother twelve white roses in a vase that changed colors the way a soap bubble does. Liberty'd smiled and hugged her, and when she pulled away, she could see tears in her mother's eyes.

Ricki gave Angel the flowers without a word. Later that night, a spring storm shook the city itself. Rain drove against the windows as the two women moved, each touch repetition and discovery. Mouths traveled, startling skin as if another unseen layer of clothing was stripped away and Ricki was truly bare for the first time. She could feel words of lust against her mouth as wind whistled against the glass, rattling the panes. She seemed to be flying, high over Angel's bed, over the studio, over the city. Higher yet, in the storm, wind and rain mixed and spilled like an ocean above the land, matching wave for wave the lakes and seas below.

Ricki stared at the cold Atlantic Ocean at Three Cliffs Bay, her muscles remembering how she'd strained back like the sea resisting the final drop to land. I hurt so bad when she was gone, that house on Banfield Street wasn't big enough to hold me. I would've been happier if she'd taken my heart, that way I wouldn't be dragging its broken pieces around with me like Liberty and that glass cat. At least that turned the whole world blue when I looked through it.

Liberty set the top and bottom halves of the cobalt cat gently back in its box. A dark rectangle in the wood of the end table marked where it had sat for so long. She sighed and looked back at her daughter. Wanting to pull Ricki close, hold her so long the sadness would slide right out of her mind and out of her hands. But Ricki, staring out the window, had the soul of a cat.

"So. You happy being that way?"

Her shoulder scarcely twitched.

"Well?"

"What's being happy, anyway?"

Ricki's voice was sharp and rippled through Liberty all out of tune. Her thighs ached with the effort of staying put. She glanced at the edge of the rug against the bare wood floor. "I want you to be happy."

"Nobody's happy, Liberty, why should I be any different?"

Because you're mine, because you're my child, my daughter. The words rang back and forth in her mind, ricocheting like light in the Hall of Mirrors.

"Do you want some coffee or something?" Ricki turned from the window and leaned on the sill.

Liberty looked up from the floor. She wanted to understand, she wanted to fill the cold emptiness in her daughter's eyes, wanted to give her as many guitars as she could play, a concert at Carnegie Hall, enough money to never worry about it and a love of her own. "So, was she good to you?"

"Who?"

"That girl. Angel."

Rickshaw turned back to the window, watching the snow swirl in circles to tie itself into a million white knots; it was so cold, it hurt to breathe. "Angel," she whispered, her heart giving a pound. Her breath fogged the glass, turning it into a flat screen of white. Against it, she could see Angel sleeping, her thick black hair scattering onto the pillow. Ricki could remember so clearly what it was like to awaken and find her body, to make love like discovering a kind of music she'd never heard before. Something beyond single notes formed beneath her hands when she touched her lover, a silent crooning lifted from them. It hurt now to think of her; Ricki's hands felt like they were glass breaking. Angel. Gone, all gone like it never happened at all.

"What happened?"

"She left. I think she thought I wasn't good enough. Or smart enough or pretty enough or something. I don't know. Could write a country music hit from her reasons."

"She thought wrong."

"Maybe. She's gone now."

"Maybe she'll come back."

Ricki shook her head.

"She with someone else?"

"Yeah." Her eyes closed and her head dropped. "Yes."

"Then good riddance to bad trash."

"She ain't trash."

"What?"

"I said, she ain't trash."

"Anybody who'd leave my daughter for someone else is trash."

Ricki turned slowly to stare at Liberty, standing there cross-armed and close-faced. Her emerald eyes clouded with tears as she turned back to the window. "She's going after someone better, Mama."

Late, late that night when only she and Tina Turner were awake, Liberty pulled out a bottle of polish and the cotton balls and walked into the kitchen. She lay down three sheets of old newspaper on the table, stuffed one hand into a tap shoe and began cleaning the gleaming patent leather. Emma? What should I do? she cried out in her mind. There was no answer, just the rattle of the window glass. Liberty pulled her sweater tighter around her, then went back to the tap shoes. You not being here turns every day harder, Emma, like a bead made out of ice. I got a collection of necklaces made from nights like this.

She wiped the top of the shoe, polishing in circles to clean it evenly. Ricki, I never wanted you to have anything but what you wanted, darling. I'd've invited her to dinner, I'd've let her spend the night, I'd've tried to talk normal and not look at her to see what's wrong and how you got trapped into it. No, baby, I didn't mean that—I don't know what I mean. I always knew there was something about Nadine and Jackie, something told me they were funny, out of focus or something. But that doesn't mean you're not right, Rickshaw Jones. You're right as rain.

She put down the left shoe and started the right. I suppose the only thing that matters is your music and picking up what's left of your heart. I'm sorry that girl hurt you, honey, I'm so sorry I can't even tell you. I wish more than anything, if she's what can make you happy she'd knock on the door right now. I'd let her in, I'd give her a cup of coffee, hell, I'd lead her to your bedroom and turn up the stereo loud as it could go to give you some privacy.

There was a hard ache between her shoulder blades as if her muscles followed her thoughts in conflict. Liberty rubbed the patent leather in slow circles. Be ready for the names, girl. Be ready for the dirt people will throw at you, no matter how good or right you are. Those words sting like a handful of glass. One will hit. Always, at least one hits its target. Maybe it's the betrayal that cuts so deep. The neighbors, their kids, the people a woman buys her food from, when she hears them whispering her privacy all around her, then the hurt is a sore beneath her skin. Something splits right open and starts to bleed. Cherise and Mamie, the underside of their skins must have been all cuts and scar tissue.

Ricki, you're looking at a life of sadness.

Black people won't want you, white people don't want you, you'll have nobody. But me. And Isra. Have you told her yet? No need, I guess, the two of you always know each other's secrets, like you been living in each other's pockets all your lives. We'll love you, she and I. With the only kind of love that counts, that's what Cherise called it.

"The kind that makes you brave for someone else, Liberty Grace." Cherise stared into ten-year-old Liberty's eyes. "You asked me once if I ever was in love. I told you yes and I'm saying it now. I am in love with that old sick woman upstairs who's going to get like poison before she finally lets go of this world. But I've loved her for thirty years and I love her still and I will sleep in that bed beside her till her pain is gone."

"But I can't, Cherise," Liberty said, eyes shining with tears she didn't want.

"If you can't find a little love for her alone, then use some that you got for me. I don't mind, I know you got plenty. Lend it to her for awhile, honey."

But I don't have to borrow love from anybody for you, Rickshaw Jones. I love you, no matter what, no matter how hard you try to make it otherwise. She finished the shoe and set it next to its partner on the newspaper. She loved the way they shined. Liberty stood up slowly, her knee twinging and the rest of her aching because of the cold. The cat rubbed against her legs and Liberty scooped her up. "What should I do, Tina Turner? Leave her be? Ricki can make her own mistakes without my help, I guess."

If I could catch up to Emma, I could tell her...Liberty let the thought go. Catching up with Emma was like trying to catch up with bright sunshine that feels like it's traveled a long way and now beats down in victory. Liberty scratched the cat's ears as she looked out the window. With the coming sun, the street rose like a stranger. I can't believe how the colors and the shapes turn into something else before the day gets here. Like a song: these blues come before dawn, long after midnight's come and gone. Look at that, maybe I'll have a mid-life career change and become a songwriter. I got plenty of blues, plenty of blues.

"Your girls are going to be teenagers soon. You ready for their rebellion?"

"I've been practicing with you all these years, I better be ready." Liberty began kneading Emma's shoulders. "You should take it easy, Emma. You don't have to keep working yourself like this."

Emma closed her eyes and let her head hang. "What do you mean? Of course I have to work."

"But not to death. Let me help you."

"There's nothing you can do. Rondo is falling apart."

"It's hard to see your own place fall apart like that."

"Well, it's not as bad as some places. It's strange, though.

Hardly nobody from the Twin Cities even lives in the neighborhood any more, they're all from somewhere else, Gary, Detroit, Chicago. It's become a real ghetto now. I'm almost happy the interstate's going through there."

"You don't mean that."

"No, I don't. I'm just tired. Come here, Tina Turner, you pretty thing." The cat curled up in Emma's lap and started to purr.

Liberty stepped around the recliner to sit on the couch. "I owe you, remember?"

Emma watched her face. Her eyes were huge. "You don't owe me, Liberty Grace."

"Let me do something."

Emma smiled softly and stroked the cat. "You've done more for me than you will ever know. You give me a safe place. You give me truth."

Liberty looked down at her folded hands, eyes closed. Her own heart seemed full of pain for a moment, as if hesitating in a beat. Soon, Liberty could feel, soon one or the other of us. She felt a warm hand cupping her chin, bringing her face up. She opened her eyes.

"You've always given me love, Liberty Grace," Emma said with a sad smile, her purple-ringed eyes filling with tears. "That's all I've ever wanted."

Liberty reached for her best friend and hugged Emma to her. God, oh, God, please don't take her, I need her, please, Liberty prayed as she gripped Emma harder. Not her, please. Then she heard Emma whisper her name and she pulled back, her hands clutching Emma's.

"Emma, darling—" A single tear like a streak of gold fell from Liberty's eye and her face tightened. "I'm afraid, Emma, I'm so afraid."

"Shh," Emma pulled her close again. "Don't be afraid. Nothing to be afraid of."

"Only the whole world. All I have is you and my girls."

"That's plenty. Plenty to live for, plenty to live with. You'll handle your fear, just like you handle everything else."

"But how can I protect them? How can I protect you?"

"You can't, honey. You have to let us all get broken sometimes."

"I don't know if I can."

"But you will. I'm telling you that you will." Emma's arms tightened around her. "I love you, Liberty Grace Jones."

"I love you, too, Emma Nevada."

"I don't know what I'd do without you. Or without this little house, this little family. Without our home."

Home—a promise made silently to each other on that hot rock near the creek way back in the childhood summers, summers filled with hard games and dance steps. A promise they kept through that first run-down apartment on Rondo back in 1958. The Penitentiary, they joked.

"More like a convent," Rita'd cracked the first time she and Billy Wayne came over, Thomas dragging along behind, on their way to Chicago with a new band. Now Billy Wayne was long dead and Thomas gone. Emma'd heard that Rita was strung out in a condemned building on the bad end of Central Avenue, less than two blocks from that old apartment.

Emma was leaving Rita's place one afternoon when a white cop pulled the trigger and she fell. The cop ran after the man who escaped over the wire fence at the other end of the alley. His white partner stopped, radioed an ambulance then looked up at the faces surrounding him. The cop holstered his gun and checked for a pulse. There was nothing. He started to sweat as the sirens screamed in his direction. The black faces above him remained as unreadable as Emma Nevada's.

Henry drove up to the house and he and Liberty went to the morgue together. Yes, that's her, she'd said, yes, that's Emma Nevada. She remembered the white man's grip on her elbow and how Henry's face closed like a door.

Liberty felt blurry from then on, as if someone or something was trying to erase her. Madame Anderhazy called; no, I won't be in, she'd said. Take as much time as you need, Madame said. Liberty stumbled her way through the next few days, feeling cold and exposed to her bones. She couldn't remember sleeping or eating, but could recall all the chores she set out to do to keep moving. Five days went by. One morning, just before the sun came up, Liberty dug the holes for the rosebushes she'd been wanting to plant since she and Emma first saw the little house.

"Needs something out front," Emma had said as she stepped around to the garage.

"Flowers?" Liberty asked, picturing marigolds and zinnias bordering the sidewalk and the driveway.

"Maybe," Emma answered. "But pick a flower with a little bit of staying power and class. Roses. Couple, three rosebushes would look fine."

It was the wrong time of year to plant them—you should plant them in late spring, not midsummer, Liberty knew, but she planted them all the same. Six bushes, buds and leaves trimmed off, roots wrapped in burlap. Isra woke up, hearing the outside faucet as Liberty watered the young plants.

"Think she's okay?" Isra whispered to Ricki as they listened to the water.

Ricki shrugged.

Next the basement was cleared. Everything not nailed down or with a specific purpose was pitched, as if all the memories attached to them could be thrown out, too. Late into the night Liberty covered the windows and began painting the cinderblock walls. Her eyes felt as if they'd been pressed against glass, but still, she could not sleep.

Liberty sat in her recliner, watching the sky grow gray-green with sunrise. The kids are asleep, the neighbors are asleep, even the damn cat is sleeping, she thought, staring down Banfield Street. She got out of the chair, a low ache in her back, and went down to the basement. Washing. Always do the washing on Tuesdays. Better soak my painting clothes, too. She kept her brain busy making grocery lists, repair lists, getting-the-house-ready-for-winter lists. I'll clear out the garage this afternoon, mow the lawn, maybe fertilize it, she thought. And better tell these damn kids they don't need three towels for every bath they take.

Liberty reached into the pile. Out came an old flannel shirt she kept meaning to return to Emma, but the cat had shed all over it and she thought it'd be nicer to get it clean first. She crushed the worn cloth in her hands. Emma. Emma gone. Emma's never coming back. Pulling the shirt to her face, she could smell her friend in the fabric, Emma's mix of sweat and spice. She invented her own colognes by wearing three different kinds. No one ever knew which or how much, but even in her radical days she couldn't give up her scent. There had even been a shoebox full of strangely shaped bottles on top of her desk, some curved so the bottom looked like hips, some oval, some cut-glass rectangles. They had been the first to go when Emma died and now they'd come back, pushing Emma Nevada to the front of Liberty's life where she had always been.

Still hugging the empty shirt, Liberty walked slowly up the stairs to her bedroom. Five days ago, me and Henry sat in that morgue looking at that husk they called Emma. Three days ago we went to the funeral, my daughters gripping my hands as if to hold me up. Now she's in the ground and I can't see her, just a stone with her name and what does a stone mean? I'd rather see Emma's ghost in this very room. But Emma died on the other side of the Mississippi River, just like Mamie, just like Cherise, and ghosts can't cross running water.

Emma. Emma Nevada.

I miss you. God, I miss you.

Liberty woke up later that day. Though the worst of the afternoon's heat had passed, it was still too warm for flannel. She pulled on Emma's shirt anyway, and walked into the kitchen to begin dinner. She cleaned up the jelly smears and toast crumbs the twins had left, and started pulling out pots and pans. My babies been eating jelly toast, she thought. Time for a decent dinner. As she gathered her children to the table, the kitchen door slammed open.

"Riot!" Big Henry panted. "People in the streets and the pigs are lining up to stop them."

Liberty moved the skillet on the stove, her back to him. "So?"

"The people are getting ready to move, woman. Our people."

"And we're getting ready to eat," she replied, turning around. "Care to join us?"

His eyes bulged. For a second, Isra was sure they'd pop right out and roll around on the floor like a pair of white tops that've run out of spin.

"You're not coming?" Henry asked.

Liberty sat in her chair and spread a napkin on her lap, smoothing the ends down. "Coming where?"

"Up to Rondo, to the streets."

"Why on god's green earth would I do that? Hand me that corn, Rickshaw, now."

Ricki passed the bowl, peering first at Liberty then up at Henry. He was so big the back porch light couldn't even shine around him.

"You aren't coming." A flat statement.

Liberty spooned out the vegetables and handed the bowl to Isra. "Be sure to eat some of these."

"The time has come, Liberty."

"Time? Time for what?" Her voice was clipped and hard.

Isra knew Henry was going to get in bigger trouble if he didn't just shut up and sit down.

"Time for us to stand against the enemy."

"The enemy. And just who, fool, is the enemy?"

"Do you want to be free?"

"Do you want to be dead?"

"Like Emma?"

"That was an accident."

"Accident? Do you think that honky pig cared when he aimed his gun?"

Liberty stabbed her fork into her hamburger and sawed at it with her knife.

"I'd rather be dead on my feet than living on my knees."

"That's a good saying, Henry. Didn't make that up by yourself, did you?"

He stared at her.

"Liberty?" Ricki slipped in.

"Here, honey, have a hamburger, go on," she answered Rickshaw. "Are you eating with us or not, Henry?" We got plenty."

"Liberty—" Ricki's voice was insistent.

His head shook. "I can't believe you're doing this."

"Doing what? Feeding my children? Rickshaw, let go of my arm and eat your dinner."

"But—"

"I can't believe you're not going. Not going to stand by the black man in his time of need."

"Is that what you call it?" Liberty twisted her wrist to break Ricki's grip. "That's what you call it when people break windows to steal out of stores—"

"That isn't what it's about."

"Yes," she hissed, "it is."

"The crimes are on whitey's head. Look what happened to Emma, it happens all over. Time for the black man to stand for himself."

Liberty stood up so quickly the chair fell back and bounced on the linoleum. "The black man?"

"We want respect," he shouted.

"Respect for what? Marching down a street chanting hate?"

"We're an oppressed people—"

"Blessed are the downtrodden, at least they got something to talk about," Liberty yelled back then walked across the kitchen to stand a foot in front of him. "You want some respect? Then look at me, Mr. Black Man. You look at my house and you look at my job and you look at my children. None of your brothers has stepped forward to educate my children, none of your brothers has volunteered to feed them or clothe them, you've given my daughters nothing."

"But we'll give them—"

"Children," she spat back. "More children, more young ones to feed to the machine, more out on the streets doing the dirty work, gassed, beat on, thrown in jail or sent to Vietnam. You mean nothing. Nothing but more dead bodies of the innocents."

"Ain't true."

Liberty walked back to her chair, set it right and sat.

"It ain't true, Liberty," he said, louder. "You know it. You're telling these children lies, Liberty."

"I want to go," Ricki piped in.

"Shut up and eat."

"But I want to go."

A vicious slap sent Rickshaw to the floor, her fork spattering grease against the wall. Big Henry was gone. Israellen stared at her mother as Liberty tried to eat as if nothing had happened. Ricki stood up, unsteady.

"One more sound—"

Rickshaw kept her eyes on her corn as she sat down, the side of her face scarlet in the shape of a hand.

"Eat!"

Ricki looked at Liberty. "Got no fork."

Liberty's eyes filled with fury. With a single sweep she was out of her chair again, throwing her plate into the sink where it crashed and shattered, leaving them alone in the kitchen.

Big Henry smelled like gasoline and sweat when he came back. "It's over," he said quietly as he walked past Liberty and into the house. "We did it."

She sighed. The sounds from the crickets lifted up and down in the grass, and the cool air touched her skin like a caress. Liberty sighed again and slowly pushed the screen door closed.

He was sitting on the couch hunched over his long legs, looking at absolutely nothing.

"What happened?"

"Cops came. A fire got started."

"That all?"

He shook his head slowly. "House burned down."

Liberty sat in her chair.

"I heard—" He stopped and cleared his throat. "There was somebody in the house."

Liberty could feel her insides shrink. The insides of my arms, she thought, the insides hurt like I should be clinging to somebody or somebody should be clinging to me.

"But we did what we said we would do."

"An eye for an eye and now we're all blind." The night dropped the temperature, but the city was caught in a heat spell of a different kind. "Burn, baby, burn. Who cares if that was a little child or an old man—"

"Stop."

A sharp pain burned into her chest and along her arm. "Stop? Stop what, telling the truth?" she asked, her question more bitter for her whispering.

"I don't want to hear the truth no more." He looked at her, the corners of his eyes red and yellow from smoke.

"You didn't want to know that throwing a brick meant someone would throw one back."

"I was angry. I wanted them to know it."

"You think white people care if we burn our own houses down? You're such a fool, you'd straddle a broomstick hoping it'll turn into a horse."

"But Emma—"

"—is dead," Liberty cried. "She is dead. I want my children to live."

"They'll live on their knees."

"No. Not my children." All of my life I been unable to look at a crowd without fear reaching to my bones. I want my children to have more than fear and hate and anger. They'll have each other. They'll have work they love and they'll have a home. I hope to give to my children—give them what Emma gave me. "Sleep, Henry. Can't fix this in one night's fighting. Sleep."

The next morning he was gone, the only sign he'd been there was the smoke Liberty was sure she could smell in the living room. She picked up the blanket on the couch and began folding it. Over once, twice, she tucked the ends in, making them square.

Ricki unfolded her sweatshirt and pulled it on. It's getting colder, Isra better get away from that water or she's going to freeze for sure. She leaned back again, watching the sun and water.

Isra stood in silence, looking out to sea. She could feel old ghosts, ghosts from people who stood on this same beach looking for lost ships or imagining what the new world would be. Maybe a hundred years from now another woman will stand here and feel our ghosts as she watches the ocean. As she watches the water, maybe I'll stand next to her holding her hand just as I am sure Liberty and Mamie and Cherise and Emma are watching me. Lost people never really lost at all. Maybe this new woman standing on this beach will have my smile. Or my hands. Maybe she'll want the sea, too, and have my way of falling in love.

Isra listened to the crash of the water. Slowly, she reached out her foot and tapped her toe on the packed sand. One, two, three, four. She tapped her heel, ball-changed to her left foot and began riffing up the beach toward her sister, scuffing her heels in the sand. She did a double-wing—right foot out, left foot out, right foot in, left foot in—not caring that the wind and sea muffled the sounds she made. She spun, her knee aching, and began riffing again.

What is she doing out there? Ricki wondered as Isra twirled again and again, shuffling through the sand.

Isra ran to the outcropping of rock. "You can hear the ocean talk. I never knew that."

"Anything will talk to you if you listen to it." She reached out her hand to help her sister up.

Isra stood on the level stone not looking at Ricki. How does it go again? she thought, tapping out the first steps of the shim-sham. Shuffle, step, shuffle, step, shuffle, ball change, shuffle, step.

"What are you doing?"

"The shim-sham." Shuffle, step, shuffle, step, shuffle, ball change, shuffle, step. She could just barely hear the sound of the dance steps on the stone. "Remember? Try it with me."

"No, I'm a terrible tap dancer."

"So what? There's nobody here to laugh at you. Get up."

"Israellen—"

Isra held out her hand. "Dance with me, Ricki. We'll just run this routine a few times and then I'll leave you alone."

Ricki grasped her hand and Isra hauled her to her feet. "I make no promises."

"Okay. Now, with your right foot: shuffle, step, shuffle, step."

Ricki copied Isra.

"Shuffle, ball change to your other foot. Good. Shuffle, step. That's the first part."

"There's more?"

"You do that three times then do the break. Take a step, slide back with your right foot, then step on your left. Do that twice."

"I don't know, Israellen."

"You're doing fine. For the last part, you jump out and back together. Just spread your legs, then slide your feet back and click your heels. Now, from the top: shuffle, step, shuffle, step—"

Ricki struggled through the routine, her face getting hot. She made it through the first step, then fell apart at the break. All that right-foot, left-foot stuff confuses me, she thought. "That's it. I give up."

"You almost had it that time."

"There's no music."

"The music's built in."

"What do you mean the music's built in?"

"What do you mean, what do I mean? The music's built in. You're the musician, Ricki, figure it out."

Rickshaw stared at Isra's feet.

Shuffle, step, shuffle, step, shuffle, ball change, shuffle, step...

"Don't watch my feet. Listen to them."

Ricki's eyes gleamed with sudden recognition. "You mean I'm supposed to *play* the routine?"

"Yes."

"Okay. Okay, then let me hear it. Just stomp really loud through the whole thing." Ricki closed her eyes as Israellen started the routine. *Shuffle, step, shuffle, step, shuffle, ball change, shuffle, step...*

Ricki bit her lip in concentration and began dancing.

Shuffle, step, shuffle, step, shuffle, ball change, shuffle, step...

"Good. You're getting it," Isra said. "Now the break: step, slide back with your right foot, step on your left."

Step, slide one foot, step on the other...

Ricki followed her.

"Then the last. Jump out, slide back and click your heels."

Jump, slide, click...

"From the top," Isra cried, her voice charged with excitement.

Shuffle, step, shuffle, step, shuffle, ball change, shuffle, step / Shuffle, step, shuffle, step, shuffle, ball change, shuffle, step...

"I got it, I got it, I got it!" Ricki shouted, her eyes wide.

Shuffle, step, shuffle, step, shuffle, ball change, shuffle, step / Step, slide one foot, step on the other / Step, slide one foot, step on the other / Jump, slide, click...

The twins danced through the routine on their shelf of stone. The sea crashed in front of them and the wind rushed over their bodies moving together in the sun.

"I've got to stop," Isra gasped. "My leg is killing me."

"Okay." Ricki danced a few more steps as if afraid to lose them, then sat down next to Israellen. "That was great. That was really great."

"You did pretty well."

"I never knew how it sounds was most important."

"That's all it is, Ricki."

The twins sat side by side. Above them, one by one in twos and threes, the gulls glided in long circles.

Rickshaw turned to her sister. Prima donna, baby sister, Israellen Jones, you are a treasure. "When are you coming home, Isra?"

"Soon, I think."

"You'll come home to me?"

Israellen looked her twin in the eye and nodded slowly. "I'll come home to you."

"Empty Bed Blues," words and music by J. C. Johnson, © 1928 by Record Music Publishing Company. All rights controlled and administered by Songwriters Guild of America, New York, New York 10001. Used by permission. All rights reserved.

"Lady Sings the Blues," words by Billie Holiday, music by Herbie Nichols, © 1956, 1972 by Northern Music Company. All rights controlled and administered by MCA Music Publishing, a Division of MCA Inc., New York, New York 10019. Used by permission. All rights reserved.

"Good Golly, Miss Molly," words and music by Robert Blackwell and John Marascalco, © 1957, 1964 by Jondora Music. All rights controlled and administered by Fantasy, Inc., Berkeley, California 94710. Used by permission. All rights reserved.

"Midnight Hour Blues," words and music by Leroy Carr, © 1962 by Leeds Music Corporation. All rights controlled and administered by MCA Music Publishing, a Division of MCA Inc., New York, NY 10019. Used by permission. All rights reserved.

"It Won't Be You," words and music by Bessie Smith. Numerous attempts to locate copyright holder(s) were unsuccessful.

"Weepin' Willow Blues," words and music by Paul Carter, © 1924 C. R. Publishing Company. All rights controlled and administered by E. T. Kirkeby, Bayonet Point, Florida 34667. Used by permission. All rights reserved.

"Are You Experienced?," words and music by Jimi Hendrix, © 1967 Bella Godiva Music, Encino Hills, CA 91436. Used by permission. All rights reserved.

"Lover Man, Oh Where Can You Be," words and music by Jimmy Davis, Roger Ramirez and Jimmy Sherman, © 1944 by Sun Music Company, Inc. All rights controlled and administered by MCA Music Publishing, a Division of MCA Inc., New York, NY 10019. Used by permission. All rights reserved.

"Amazing Grace," Deep River," "Ezekiel Saw the Wheel," "Oh, Freedom," and "This Train" are traditional songs.

224